Acclaim

WAR & WARM FUZZIES is a thought-provoking read from beginning to end with many messages, directly stated or subtly implied, to be interpreted by the reader. The over-all crux of the story was, for me, how sad it is that after generations of wars, fought under the banners of religion, race and political gain, lessons and attitudes have changed little. When I think about the current troubles of our world I feel that we appear to have learned little and continue to replicate the attitudes and errors of the past. The moral of the story was clear to me, if we fail to find the inner love for our fellow humans, irrespective of race or creed, then we fail ourselves and ultimately "The Great I Am". In the words of Nelson Mandela "No one is born hating another person because of the color of his skin, or his background, or his religion. People must learn to hate, and if they can learn to hate, they can be taught to love, for love comes more naturally to the human heart than its opposite." (Robert Smith Duncan: Musician, Singer, Actor (TV and Film) and Psychic Counselor)

WAR & WARM FUZZIES is the best explanation I have ever read, as to why we are trapping ourselves in the endless cycle of war and hatred. We all have the seeds of love and hate within us, and it is our choice which seed we want to water. In this story, we witness two friends struggling with that choice between light and darkness, love and hate. This is one of those simple messages that could truly change the world we live in, if we only woke up to the truth about love and human kindness. This is truly a feel-good book. (Paul Richards, Actors' Equity Association, as Ranko in the original cast of the play "Warm Fuzzies" in 1994-95.)

I agree that the timing of a book on this theme is perfect now. (Mark Blomberg: as Rakic in the original cast of the play "Warm Fuzzies" in 1994-95.)

WAR & WARM FUZZIES is a graphic and touching story about how 2 boys get unintentionally involved in a political mess; how the nature of politics is to indoctrinate and divide people; how philanthropists are punished by criminals and religious propaganda. The book vividly describes how evil roots itself in doubt and suspicion, but also that love and kindness can prevail by will. (Delila: the daughter of a refugee family from the Bosnian war)

The drawings and puppets shown in this book are taken from the original theatrical production of *WARM FUZZIES*. They are the work of **Krister Åsard.**

WAR & WARM FUZZIES©
By
Richard P. Matthews

Revitalizing Ministries
Hill, New Hampshire

PUBLISHED BY REVITALIZING MINISTRIES
Copyright © 2015 by Richard P. Matthews

Published in the United States by Revitalizing Ministries, Hill, New Hampshire.
www.RevitaizingMinistries.com
The portrayal of the embossed leaf with Revitalizing Ministries is a registered trademark of Revitalizing Ministries.

Library of Congress Control Number: 2007932585
Matthews, Richard P.
War and Warm Fuzzies/Richard P. Matthews.—1st ed.
p. cm.
1. War and Warm Fuzzies—Fiction. 2. Action Adventure,
3. Historical Fiction, 4. Science Fiction, 5. Fantasy,
6. Military History, 6. World History
I. Title. II. Matthews, Richard P.

ISBN 973-0-9798106-5-7

PRINTED IN THE UNITED STATES OF AMERICA

10   8   6   4   2   1   3   5   7   9

CONTENTS

6

INTRODUCTION

The story told here was originally written as a play, "Warm Fuzzies," in Sweden during 1993-94. The war in Bosnia-Herzegovina was in full swing. The play was produced in 1994 and toured Sweden in September of that year, with its premier in Lund. The pictures of the Fairytale in this book were part of that production. Also, some of the members of the cast and crew were refugees from the war, which did not end until 14 December 1995. The picture on the front cover of this book is the before and after picture of the library in Konjic.

While the events and characters in this story are purely fictitious, the actual senseless atrocities and human behavior in all wars is portrayed here in graphic detail. Hopefully people will react on the level of the violence, but understand that it has been toned down compared to what really happens in war. There is no glory or honor in any war, and the "war to end all wars" is more of a myth than any fairy tale. The real heroes that survive any war are not the medal winners, but those who work tirelessly to end all war and hatred.

In the Fairytale, "Warm Fuzzies," (originally written in the early 1950s) the basic truth of love and human kindness is the real magic in every human heart. Those that choose to believe the lie of the Wicked Witch are the perpetrators of every war or human conflict. Those that empty their bag of "Warm Fuzzies" every day are our only hope for any kind of a decent life now.

CHAPTER 1
Best Friends

There is only peace and quiet before dawn. Then all of nature seems to come alive. The star studded sky starts to turn gray. A breeze starts to rustle through the trees. The birds stretch their wings as the yellow rays of sunshine peak over the horizon.

It is August 1990 in Konjic, Bosnia-Herzegovina. We are in the beautiful mountains overlooking Lake Boračko. We soar like a golden eagle over the land. The sun breaks forth proudly over the mountaintops surrounding the lake. The lush green trees are crowned with the golden light that slips slowly down the mountain slopes to dance across the quiet water, whose smooth resting surface is disturbed only by a jumping feeding fish. The hillside slowly comes to life, bathed in beauty, gloriously painted by Mother Nature's brush. Bird songs begin to fill the air. All is tranquil. All is in order. All is at peace. In the distance, the small village of Konjic has yet to waken to greet the day. It lies peacefully on both sides of the Neretva River that springs from the lake. Slowly we circle a small tent almost hidden by the undergrowth. It sits peacefully nestled into the hillside a few meters above the lake.

Two fourteen-year-old boys lie in their sleeping bags. Jusuf and Vladimir have been best friends most of their lives. There is a deep and enduring bond between them.

Vladimir is awake, but lying in his North Face down sleeping bag with his hands behind his head.

His face is tranquil, with youthful thoughts of everything in general and nothing in particular. He is a good looking boy, with strong features and bright eyes.

Jusuf is starting to wake up. He rolls and tries to stretch, fighting the bulk and stiffness of his Dacron filled sleeping bag. His long black hair is splayed out across his makeshift pillow, which is his rolled up jeans. His face is thin, with soft delicate features, which gives him a kind and welcoming appearance. Slowly, he opens his eyes and rubs them with the palms of his hands. He announces, "The sun's up."

"No kidding, Sherlock." Vladimir laughs and smiles at his friend.

They start to get out of their sleeping bags, which is all asses and elbows in the small tent.

"You were already awake?" Jusuf asks.

Vladimir yawns and stretches, "Yea, the birds."

Jusuf dives back in his bag, "The bears!"

Vladimir whacks him with a dirty sock and laughs, "The BIRDS, dummy! You know, tweet, tweet."

They both laugh hysterically.

The Boys emerge from the tent and finish adjusting their clothes.

While they start a fire for breakfast, Vladimir begins to laugh as he remembers an embarrassing moment. "Do you remember last Christmas, when we went into that lingerie shop in the village, so that I could buy a bra for my girlfriend?"

"God, you embarrassed me," Jusuf says. "You picked out the sexiest, laciest and lowest-cut bra you could find."

Jusuf starts to cook their breakfast.

Vladimir pantomimes his actions as he holds up the imaginary bra and strokes the soft delicate lace with his dancing fingers. He pauses over where the nipples would be and massages that area gently. He starts to moan with pleasure.

Jusuf is soon hysterical with laughter,

Vladimir asks, "Do you remember how we figured out the cup size?"

Jusuf blushes, "Oh, no!"

Vladimir says, "You held up the bra to your chest, and I eyeballed it and cupped my hand over it."

They are laughing so hard, they don't hear a loud pop from the fire, or see the puff of smoke and a large flying ember. It lies smoldering in the grass.

As the fire continues to spit and sputter with sparks flying in every direction, the two boys jump and dodge the hot sparks and then settle down again to the story and breakfast.

Vladimir's pantomiming becomes more risqué as he describes what he did with Jusuf and the bra.

Jusuf remembers, "But the real question was whether or not you had any firsthand experience."

Vladimir laughs, "Yea, HAND experience, a little touchy-feely, a little kissy-face and huggy-bear, but nothing more than HAND experience."

They are totally unaware as the fire catches in the dry grass and begins its dance. At first, it is small, smoldering and smoking, and then it bursts into flames. The Boys are so intent on their story that they don't notice what is happening behind them.

Jusuf says, "It took thirty minutes and fifty-two attempts to get up enough nerve to go check out."

The fire dances out of control and becomes more intense, catching hold and burning with greater and greater strength.

Vladimir says, "Then I held up the bra to you and said that you would look very good in it."

The fire begins to spread.

Jusuf is now red as a beet, "I melted into the floor cracks when I saw the sales clerk watching us."

The Boys laugh uproariously. In the middle of their laughter, Vladimir roles to the ground and sees the fire, which is now totally out of control. He jumps up and takes his towel and tries to beat it out. Jusuf does the same. All their efforts only fan the fire into a bigger blaze. Jusuf thinks fast and runs and picks up two cook pots and hands one to Vladimir, who looks at him confused, with his mouth open.

Jusuf says urgently, "We have to throw water on the fire!" He runs down to the lake, fills the pot, races back to the fire and throws it into the blaze.

Vladimir gets the idea and springs into action. They rush back and forth from the lake to the fire dousing it with the water. At first, it looks hopeless and overwhelming, but then they slowly bring the fire under control. At that point, their panic shifts to humor and their racing back and forth becomes a comical dance to subdue the fire.

Jusuf can't resist asking, "By the way, whatever happened to that girlfriend? Did you ever see her in the bra?"

Vladimir swears under his breath and then says, "Just after Christmas, we broke up and she started going out with Ivo. He took her to the New Year's Eve party."

"Ivo the dork! She probably wore the bra and showed it to him."

"I'll never have another girlfriend...," Vladimir says, and then adds, "...who wears bras."

They both laugh hysterically. Finally, they succeed in putting the fire out, and then they pick up the large smoldering sticks, carry them down to the lake and throw them in.

Jusuf congratulates Vladimir, "Nice work, Ace. We better look around to make sure nothin' else is left smoldering."

As they start to check the area, Vladimir finds something.

Vladimir is elated, "Look here under this bush! It's an old German SS helmet from WW II.

Jusuf holds up the palm of his hand and turns his head away. "That's a time best forgotten. Come on, let's break camp and head home."

They roll up their sleeping bags and stuff all their gear into their knapsacks. They fold up the tent, and start their trek back to Konjic.

Vladimir's mood changes, and there is a long silence between them. Vladimir's face becomes taut. His eyes are distant. His shoulders slump forward. He dreads every step he takes. He keeps turning back

toward their campsite and the lake. Then with a deep
sigh, he turns and races to catch up to Jusuf.

Jusuf is smiling, and joy fills his body. There
is a spring to his step. As he looks around and takes in
the spectacular vista, it takes his breath away followed
by a deep inhale and a sigh of satisfaction. To him all
the world is at peace and his life is perfectly tranquil.

As they hike down a treacherous section of the
trail, with a sheer drop-off, Vladimir is the first to
break the silence. "God, this trail is narrow!"

Jusuf doesn't look down, "Just don't fall down
there."

Vladimir stares at the long drop, "No way! I
don't want to be bird food and fish bait."

There is a long silence between them again.
As they hike down the trail it widens a bit, but there is
still a sheer drop.

Vladimir finally reveals what is bothering him.
He takes a deep breath, and the words tumble out of
his mouth, like birds escaping a cage, "You know, I
really don't want to go home."

"How come?"

Vladimir slowly opens up, but you can hear
the pain in his voice. "Things are worse since my
Grandpa moved up to Sarajevo, to start his political
career. The parties this summer have been totally out
of control. In fact, one morning I woke up to find a
naked woman in bed with me."

Jusuf spins around with a dumbfounded
expression on his face, "What? You're kidding."

"No, for true." Vladimir crosses his heart and
holds up his right hand, as in taking an oath.

Jusuf reacts jovially, "Sounds great. Did you get a good look?"

Vladimir doesn't laugh; he is too sensitive about it.

Now, Jusuf senses Vladimir's pain. He becomes compassionate and serious, "I'm sorry. I know it's tough on you, but you have to put it out of your mind. Your parents are what they are, and there is nothing you can do that will ever change them."

Vladimir sighs, "I wish I had parents like yours."

Jusuf jokingly replies, "Great, I'll sell 'em to you."

They both laugh.

Vladimir's mood improves for a while. Then he starts to examine the SS helmet. It really fascinates him, or he is drawn to something about it. It is not old enough to be an antique, but to him it is precious and not in a good way. It is precious more like the ring is precious to Gollum in *Lord of the Rings*. He slowly and unconsciously strokes it as he is walking along the trail. He holds it tightly to his chest. After a while, he comes to a complete stop to admire it. Jusuf is unaware and walking on ahead. They are over fifty meters apart when Jusuf finally speaks to Vladimir.

"Are you thirsty?"

When there is no answer, he turns and sees Vladimir stroking the helmet. He walks back. When he is ten meters away Vladimir looks up. His eyes appear to be glazed and fixed.

Vladimir says in a mechanical tone, "I think I'll try out this SS helmet." He puts the helmet on reverently and salutes, "heil Hitler." There is a personality change in Vladimir and a very different tone in his voice. He approaches Jusuf, who starts to back up. "O.K., you Jew bastards keep moving. I don't give a damn how dangerous it is." It is not clear if he is talking to Jusuf or some phantom person. Then he turns to some imagined person on his right, "What did you say, bitch? Speak up?" He spins back to Jusuf, "I heard that, you stinkin' Jew!" Now, he seems to be talking to many imagined people standing on the trail, "O.K., all of you line up on the ledge."

Vladimir pretends to line up a group of Jews at gun point.

Jusuf is cowering away. "What are you doing?"

Vladimir points his imaginary weapon at Jusuf. "Stand up, you stupid Jew boy!"

He forces Jusuf over to the edge.

Vladimir shouts, "Get in line!"

He starts at the far end from Jusuf and shoots the first one. He walks to the edge and looks down. He laughs maniacally. "Look, his head broke open like a watermelon. His brains are all over the rocks."

Then he steps back and shoots the others one at a time. With each one, he laughs more hideously until his laughter is almost inhuman. When he comes to Jusuf he sticks the imaginary gun in his face.

Jusuf is terrified. "What's happening?!"

There is a maniacal look on Vladimir's face. For a moment, the Boys are frozen in this scene of terror. Suddenly, Vladimir rips off the helmet. His personality changes back immediately. He tries to comfort Jusuf, holding his face.

"It's O.K. I was just fooling around. It was just a game."

Jusuf moves away from the edge, trying to shake it off. "Some game! You almost killed me."

Vladimir says meekly, "I don't know what got into me."

They continue down the trail in silence for several minutes.

Finally, Jusuf says, "I don't like that helmet. It frightens me."

Vladimir rationalizes, "It's just an old helmet, there's nothing to be afraid of."

Jusuf turns, "There is only one person who can say that for sure, and that is Nedjo. Look, here's the fork to his place. Let's take it to him and ask him to do a reading on it."

Vladimir tries to change the subject, "I vote we go to your place. I'm too tired to climb up there. Your mom'll have something for us to eat."

Jusuf is decisive, "Look, you should either destroy the helmet or take it to Nedjo to get a reading on it. Which will it be?"

Vladimir strokes the helmet. "It's too valuable to destroy! Besides, it's just a harmless helmet."

Jusuf presses the issue, "Then what do you have against the Jews in the village?"

Vladimir caves, "O.K.! O.K.! We take the helmet to Nedjo. The Gypsy will agree with me."

They start to climb the steep trail up to Nedjo's house and workshop.

CHAPTER 2
The Reading

Nedjo's workshop and home are at the top of a mountain overlooking Konjic. There are no utility services. Yet he has solar electrical power, running water, and independent cell phone and internet connections. It is not accessible by car. Yet there is a secret underground cable tram down to the bus stop on the highway. Nedjo is the only one who knows about it.

Shelves fill the walls of his workshop, which actually cover all the windows. The shelves are stuffed full of small wooden storage boxes, a little smaller than a shoe box. A paper tag hangs from each box. In addition to the small boxes, there are three large wooden storage bins. These are not tagged. In orderly piles all over the floor there sit disassembled devices of every kind imaginable. In the center of the room is a large workbench, with a ten centimeter thick solid wood top. The bench and room are exceptionally orderly.

Nedjo is sitting at the workbench fiddling with an electronic device. He is very virile-looking and appears to be in his early sixties, but in reality is 84+. His hair is snow white, and his face is ruddy and kind.

Nedjo is one of Konjic's very special people. He has been 90% blind from birth. He is one of very few people, who managed to survive the social polarity of Communism. He has no privileges or state income in spite of his handicap, and yet he lives very comfortably.

He works as an inventor. His home and workshop are filled with these gadgets and creations. He has patented and sold many of his inventions. However, he is very secretive about his work, because he has had two of his inventions stolen. They were his only weapons inventions, so he refuses to do any more work for the military. His favorite expression is, "If a rose had not already been created, I would invent it; because you cannot kill a person with a rose." At this very moment, Nedjo looks up from his work and smiles as though he just felt you read his rose quote.

Nedjo is busy working at his bench on what he calls the Fairytale device.

It is late morning when the Boys reach Nedjo's workshop. Jusuf and Vladimir enter the door to the workshop. It is obvious that they have been there many times before. They look at each other and make a sign. Then they start to walk with a different step. Jusuf walks with a very heavy step, and Vladimir walks with a limp dragging one foot. They weave their way through a maze of gadgets, machinery and devices until they come to where Nedjo sits.

Nedjo says without looking up, "Good morning, Jusuf, Vladimir."

Jusuf says to Vladimir, "How did he know it was us?"

Vladimir says to Nedjo, "We disguised our steps."

Nedjo chuckles, "I have other senses."

Jusuf smells his arm pits, "Do we smell that bad?"

Nedjo laughs. "No. Fact is you smell like a couple of smoked sausages."

Vladimir leans in, "How then?"

Nedjo explains while continuing to work. "There is a sixth sense, which is higher than all the others are. I knew you were coming twenty minutes ago, when you chose to take the path to my place."

The Boys are dumb-founded as they look at each other. Then they shrug their shoulders and turn to look at what Nedjo is doing.

"What's that?" Jusuf asks.

"A Fairytale device."

Vladimir scratches his head. "A what?"

Nedjo continues, "Instead of just watching a tape of a Fairytale, the device lets you go into it and experience it first-hand."

Jusuf examines it more closely. "Wow. How does it work?"

Nedjo patiently shows them the details of the Fairytale device. The Boys are in awe.

"They may look like a pair of oversized goggles, but it's really a high-tech headset. These electrodes rest on the temples and load the story into the mind. Inside here are two baby TV screens. You can see normally through the tinted goggles, but when the TV screens are on, they blend with what you see in reality. So you have the illusion that you are inside the TV image."

Vladimir interjects, "This would be great for computer games."

"Maybe, but I don't like computer games. They're too violent and make you tense. I prefer Fairytales." He holds up a computer disc about the size of a bottle cap. This miniature video disc is the one I'm working on. It's called 'Warm Fuzzies' and teaches people the importance of love and kindness to each other."

Jusuf is getting excited. "Can we try it?"

"There's a problem. Once you get into the Fairytale, you can't get out. It seems to be loaded into the subconscious mind somehow, so when you take off the headset the subconscious mind can send you back into the Fairytale any time it wants."

"I can wait," says Vladimir hesitantly.

Nedjo becoming lost in his own thoughts for a moment, "I'm sure it has something to do with the electric sensors and the computer, as it loads the story into the RAM memory, thus interfacing with the real memory of the user. When the program is logged off in the shutdown, it downloads only the RAM memory without off-loading the memory of the user. But that poses another problem, because we don't want to erase the total memory of the user, do we?" He comes back to the Boys. "It's only a small problem. I'll fix it."

The Boys are confused and react together, "Say what?"

Nedjo turns to the Boys, "Haven't you forgotten the real reason you came here?"

Vladimir is surprised, "How did you know that?"

The two boys look at each other puzzled.

"Well, Vladimir found this ..." Jusuf starts, but

Vladimir cuts him off, being very protective. "I can tell him."

Vladimir puts on the helmet again, and again his personality changes. He starts to ask Nedjo very personal questions in a strange voice.

He is accusing and threatening, "Gypsy, is it true you aided American pilots during the war? Do you have a secret room in this house? Whose side are you on?"

Nedjo turns to Jusuf. "There are two demons around the helmet. They are hideous smoke like creatures. They have control of him when he puts it on."

Jusuf reacts, "I can't see a thing."

Nedjo starts to shout at the demons. "I call you out, Seth and Wormwood. *Sabiath votalime het iranomus bayoo*! Be Gone! BE GONE!"

Vladimir falls to the floor and convulsions seizes him.

Jusuf is concerned, "What's happening? Is he going to die?"

"The demons are frightened." Nedjo continues in a large commanding voice, "*Iranomus bayoo! IRANOMUS BAYOO!* BE GONE! I call thee by name, Seth and Wormwood. BE GONE!"

With a loud crash and screech, the demons leave him. Vladimir comes back to himself, while lying on the floor. He takes off the helmet but continues to hold it tenderly.

Vladimir looks up at Nedjo and Jusuf, "I feel funny."

Jusuf turns to Nedjo, "What does it mean?"

Nedjo summarizes, "The demons I saw in the helmet have been temporarily scared off. But you can be sure they will be back, because the helmet is theirs and they control whoever wears it."

Vladimir quickly pitches the helmet to Jusuf, who throws it back.

Vladimir throws it aside, like a hot potato.

Jusuf is still concerned, "What do we do?"

Nedjo explains, "You take it to the junk yard and throw it into the compactor. Then it will be melted down once and for all."

Vladimir is frightened, "We'll do it on the way home."

The Boys start to leave. Nedjo looks up and away. He sees something in the Boys' future, and calls out to them. "Jusuf, Vladimir, just a minute."

It is obvious that he is concerned about something he sees in their lives.

Jusuf turns, "What is it?"

Nedjo thinks better of it, "Never mind, it was nothing. Be careful and come back real soon."

The Boys leave and start down the trail to Konjic. Vladimir will not carry the helmet. He ties a piece of string to it and drags it along behind him. However, all he can talk about is his experience with the demons.

He says, "I had no idea that demons could take me over and make me do whatever they wanted. It is like I had no control over what I was doing. I didn't even think it was me. It is terrible. I feel so violated."

Jusuf stops and turns to him. "Look, you have to put it out of your head and focus on something positive. When we get home, my mom will have some food for us."

"That's it. I'll focus on your mom's cooking. You have the best mom in the whole world."

The Boys make a beeline for the town dump.

CHAPTER 3
Divide & Conquer

Late that same morning, Ranko, Vladimir's father and his grandfather, Rakic, are stacking crates in a large underground bunker. It is a secret storage bunker inside a mountain on the Rakic estate. In this large bunker are stored arms of all types that have been illegally appropriated or purchased in secret arms deals. The older intense-looking man is General Rakic, the owner of the estate and a retired General from the Yugoslavian army. When he retired from the military in 1988 he moved to Sarajevo to pursue his political career and organize a Serbian state militia in Bosnia-Herzegovina. Now, as the leader of the Serbian Party, he is actively campaigning for president of the new republic of Bosnia-Herzegovina.

The slick-looking younger man with him is his son Ranko, who now lives on the estate with his family. He is one of the five Directors at the Igman arms factory. There is no higher position in the company or the community.

The arms crates they are off-loading are Ranko's most recent appropriation from the arms factory. The bunker is just about packed to capacity.

Ranko explains while he is carrying an arms crate, "The badges would look like American campaign buttons for the different parties. They would identify the wearer as Serbian, Croatian, Muslim or Communist, creating a feeling of political pride and personal identity. You get the idea?"

They off-load the last crate as Rakic responds. He is greatly impressed. "Yes, and I like it. Very clever, you're a chip of the old block. Do we have time to have them made?"

Ranko smiles enthusiastically, "I knew you would go for it. Come and look."

He leads him to a stack of cardboard boxes off to the side. He breaks open four of them and shows him the buttons.

Rakic complements him, "That's what I like, initiative."

Ranko is puffed up by the praise, "This one is the Serbian button, this one Croatian, this one Muslim and this one the Communists. Am I brilliant or what?

Laughing, Rakic says, "Congratulations, son, a very clever idea. How kind of you to think of everybody. And I can see exactly where you're going with it. Divide and conquer. Let's load 'em up."

They start to load the boxes onto the tuck as Rakic explains, "You know they must be distributed secretly. After all, you don't want them to know who their generous benefactors might be. Of course, I will come out publicly against them. The Serbian party will be the unifying party. What a fantastic idea!"

Ranko responds, "O.K. I can get half the buttons out through the schools."

Rakic adds, "And I'll plant the other half with the different campaign headquarters." They load the last box, and Rakic turns to Ranko, "That's everything. We're out a here."

They climb into the truck and pull out; as the truck clears the entrance, a large door slides into place. It looks exactly like part of the cliff wall. It would never be noticed, even on close examination.

CHAPTER 4
Homecoming

Meho, Jusuf's father, is working in his cabinet shop. It is on the ground floor of their home. He is a 45-year-old short stocky man with a kind and open face. Meho is the seventh generation of Muslim cabinetmakers and woodcarvers to run this small business for the past 120 years. He only makes a modest living from his work even though his woodcarvings are renowned.

He is struggling with a repair on his old band saw, which is almost twice as old as he is, as are most of the tools in the shop. He talks to it like it were his child, needing love and discipline.

"Now get in there, and behave yourself. Come on ... Come on ... There you go." There is no anger, just firmness.

The Boys nosily enter through the shop door talking about the huge metal compactor.

Vladimir says, "I crushed the helmet and that whole car like a mud pie."

They take off their backpacks and set them down.

Jusuf greets his father, "Hi, Papa."

Meho backs out of the small access hole in the band saw and stands up. "Welcome home, mountain man."

Jusuf goes to his father and gives him a hug. Vladimir looks on. "Hi, Meho."

Meho says to Vladimir, "Hi, son" and shakes his hand vigorously.

Meho goes back to his repair job and squeezes into the access hole.

Jusuf asks, "Can I help?"

"Hand me the large wrench there. How was the camping trip? Did you catch any fish?

Jusuf hands his father the wrench. Vladimir starts to sweep up the shop.

Jusuf answers, "We had fish every night for dinner, but it wasn't enough to feed a kitten, let alone Vladimir."

Vladimir reacts, "What do you mean! I don't eat half of what you pack away."

Meho laughs, "I can agree with that. He eats the most in the whole family."

Jusuf gently kicks the bottom of his father's boot.

What we are about to see is an old routine that Vladimir has been doing since he has been getting an allowance. While the others are occupied with the machine, Vladimir opens the shop cash box. It is empty. He takes some money out of his pocket, counts it and puts it into the shop cash box. He then goes about his sweeping. Of course, Meho has been wise to this for years, but never says anything. After a day or two, he simply gives the money to Jusuf, and suggests that he take Vladimir to the movies. Remember this later in the story, that this is who Vladimir really is.

Meho asks Jusuf, "Hand me the hammer."

"The big one or little one?"

Meho considers for a moment, "Better make it the big one."

Jusuf hands his father the hammer. Just then, Aisha, Jusuf's mother, opens the door from the house and comes into the shop. She is a strong attractive woman from old peasant stock. She is 44, with a pleasant, inviting and friendly appearance.

Aisha puts her hands on her hips and says to the Boys, "Well, well, look whose back! I thought I heard voices down here. Welcome back to civilization. Come give us a hug."

She greets the Boys and hugs them both. She sniffs them trying to identify the smells on them.

Jusuf responds affectionately, "Hi, Mama."

Vladimir also greets her warmly, "Nice to see you, Aisha."

Aisha asks, "What's that smell?"

Vladimir responds, "We had to put out a fire in the woods this morning. It isn't that bad, is it?"

Aisha reacts, "I can't let you go home smelling like that. Get out of those clothes, and I'll wash them."

The Boys look at each other in embarrassment.

Vladimir protests, "Say what?"

Jusuf joins in, "Mama!"

Aisha smiles, "Come on. You don't have anything I haven't seen before." Turning to Vladimir, "Besides, you go home smelling like that, your mom will be back with them tomorrow."

They strip down to their underwear while Aisha looks on. Then they stop.

Aisha insists, "Those too."

The Boys say together, "No way!"

Aisha and Meho laugh, but the Boys' embarrassment goes through the roof.

Aisha says, "If you must, take them off upstairs, and Jusuf, give Vladimir something to put on."

The Boys quickly go up into the house. Aisha walks over to Meho, as he stands up. She gives him a kiss and then walks to the door to the house.

Meho watches her with a grin on his face, "Do you want to wash my clothes too?"

Aisha turns back, "You're just looking for an excuse to take them off."

Meho says innocently, "Who, me?"

"Yes, you. You're just a horny old man."

"After 26 years of marriage, you're still the most beautiful woman in town."

Aisha winks seductively, "Tonight!"

She slowly closes the door behind herself.

CHAPTER 5
Oh, the Badges

A few days later in the late afternoon, Nedjo is in his kitchen. He is sitting at the kitchen table sipping a cup of coffee and reading a Braille book. Suddenly the Boys burst into the kitchen. They are out of breath and can hardly speak.

Jusuf pants out, "Nedjo... Can we..."

Vladimir blurts out almost at the same time, "Sorry ... to burst... in... like this."

"What is it?" Nedjo says calmly.

The Boys start to speak simultaneously.

Jusuf says, "It was awful!"

Vladimir says, "I'm scared! My father'll kill me."

Nedjo stands and takes a deep breath, which has a calming effect on the Boys. "Sit down, just calm yourselves. I'll fix you a cup of hot chocolate. Don't say another thing until you have taken three deep breaths."

The Boys sit down and start to breathe. Nedjo starts to fix the hot chocolate. He is moving about the kitchen like a sighted person, with only a few hints of his vision impairment, like putting his finger inside the cup when pouring.

Nedjo turns to the Boys, "O.K. One at a time. Tell me what happened."

The Boys are calmer now, but they rattle off their experiences in a rapid succession, without pause or hesitation.

Vladimir starts. "Just after school, I was walking down the corridor to meet Jusuf, when a group of older Serbian students approached me and asked me to put on a Serb badge.

Jusuf adds, "It was like a contest to see who could get rid of the most badges."

Vladimir says, "I told the guy I didn't see the point, but he said that they were for my Grandfather's and Father's party. So I took one of the badges and pinned it on. They shook my hand and congratulated me and moved on to the next student. Then I saw Jusuf down the hall, and another group was after him."

"The Muslims tried to push a Muslim badge off on me. I told them that I wasn't political, and that things like this could divide the people ethnically. Why can't we just be friends? Then a shouting match began, and the older students started to threaten me. Their fun turned ugly in a flash."

Nedjo puts the cups down in front of them and sits down at the head of the table.

Vladimir fires out, "When the older students tried to force the badge on Jusuf, he ripped it off and threw it to the ground."

"I told him it's not right, and I knew it'd come to no good."

Vladimir stands and starts to act out what happened. "By this time the other ethnic groups joined the mobbing and Jusuf was being singled out like a hostile enemy. Then a tough upper-level Serb took a Muslim badge and tried to force him to wear it.

"I said, 'You like it. You wear it!'"

"The Serb drove a hard punch into Jusuf's gut." Jusuf reacts. "Jusuf curled up. The Serb came up with his knee in Jusuf's face. Jusuf went flying back, sprawling on the floor. I was on the outside trying to get in. I leaped into the air."

"He came flying over the crowd and landed on top of the Serb, taking him down. He sat on top of the big kid and pounded away at his face. The others tried to stop him; three older students went flying. The crowd backed off. When the Serb got up..."

Vladimir inserts. "He shook his fist at Jusuf and said, 'I'm going to kill you, you little turd.'"

Jusuf says, "But Vladimir stepped between us and said, 'He's my friend! Leave him alone!' Then he ripped off his badge and threw it in his face. The Serb started for him, but Vladimir came up with a swift kick to the guy's groin. He doubled over and fell to his knees in pain."

Vladimir says, "Just then, two teachers and an administrator pushed their way through the crowd and took hold of us. They were wearing the badges."

Jusuf says, "They took us to the headmaster's office."

The Boys finally take a breath.

Nedjo asks, "What did you tell the headmaster?"

Jusuf says with conviction, "We both refused to wear them. I'm not afraid of what my father will say, because I know he's not political.

Vladimir is more hesitant, "But I'm terrified at what my father will do; and worse yet, The General is going to take it as a personal insult."

Nedjo pauses and takes a deep breath. "Look, for what it's worth, I think you did the right thing, and I'm proud of you. This whole election business is out of hand. The candidates are like a married couple. One says an ugly word about the other, so the other person has to find an even uglier word to throw back. Once enough ugly words are said the marriage falls apart. You must lead your friends toward a more positive way of thinking."

The Boys sit back and take a breath.

Then Jusuf asks, "Sure, but how do we do that?"

Vladimir leans forward, "How do we become leaders? Everyone's against us now."

Nedjo stands and crosses to the stove. He picks up the hot chocolate pot and comes back to the table. The Boys watch him as he carefully pours more hot chocolate in the cups, without spilling a drop. He sets the empty pot down on a trivet.

Nedjo picks up his cup and starts to walk into the living room. "I once heard a riddle about leadership. If you can solve the riddle, you can answer your own questions.

The Boys look at each other. Then without a word, they grab their cups and stand up.

Jusuf is eager, "Come on. He's going to tell a story."

Vladimir is hesitant, "O.K., but I need more than a story right now!"

The Boys follow Nedjo into the living room. They watch as Nedjo takes something down from the bookshelf. He then hands the Boys an ancient scroll with hieroglyphics on it. As the Boys unroll the scroll, Nedjo walks over to his easy chair and sits.

The Boys sit on the floor in front of his chair, just as they have done for many stories in years past.

Nedjo and the Boys take a sip of their hot chocolate and Nedjo begins. The Boys follow along with the scroll.

"In ancient times a great land was without a leader. The king had died and left no heir to the throne. So they searched the kingdom both far and wide to find a leader: a leader who was wise, selfless and understanding. A leader who would love the people so they would trust and follow.

"Then came a young lad and stood before the council. They examined him for three days, but they could not agree. So they decided on a test to see if the lad was capable of leading them. They gave him three smoked fish and a loaf of bread and sent him up into the mountains to pass the test that the 'Great I Am' would present to him within thirty days and thirty nights.

"In late January the lad went up into the mountains. His food did not last long, and the coldest and foulest winter in the history of the land blew over the mountains.

"After twenty eight days he was starving to death and both his feet were frozen, for his shoes had cracked and broken away in his wandering. He huddled under a great pine tree pulling the boughs in around him, and there he prayed, but the 'Great I Am' was not speaking to him. The next morning he trudged out into the snow to continue the search for the 'Great I Am's test. As the day passed, the wind tried to cut him in two. The snow tried to blind his eyes, and he thought that he would surely perish this night. He was out of time, out of strength and almost out of hope. Then he heard a faint sound of a lamb crying. He followed the sound until he came to a steep cliff. There he looked down and saw a wolf dragging a crying lamb."

"This was the test."

The Boys look up and wait for a long moment. They look at the scroll and then look back at Nedjo.

Vladimir breaks the silence, "What did he do?"

Jusuf adds, "Go on!"

Nedjo explains, "You must search for the answer yourselves. For only a true leader will find the right answer to the riddle. If you are to lead, you will find the answer yourselves."

CHAPTER 6
Twisted Abuse

Like everything in this story, nothing is ever what it seems to be. It is the middle of the night. There is no light coming in any window of the library on the Rakic Estate. All we can hear is their breathing.

Darkness! Is it a quiet place of peace and solitude, or a frightening place of danger and terror? Which darkness is it that we find in the library of the Rakic Estate? Sitting in this darkness is Vladimir's beautiful Croatian mother, Ana. She is a 39-year-old exceptionally attractive woman, who is well trained and athletic-looking. With her is General Jovanovic, Vladimir's great-grandfather, who is now retired from the Serbian army. He is 61, rough and powerful-looking, but with the beginnings of a paunch belly. In the darkness, listen and form your own opinions.

Ana screams, "Yhaaaaaaa...!"

A loud slap is heard as a hand strikes flesh.

Jovanovic shouts, "Shut up!"

Ana pleads, "Please don't hurt me! What do you want from me?"

Jovanovic says in a powerful voice, "You know what I want."

Ana is whimpering and groaning as we hear the repeated slapping and pounding of human flesh. There is the sound of tearing fabric, ripping apart and a shoe falling to the floor.

Ana screams, "No, no, no, No!"

Jovanovic laughs and strikes again, and again, and again.

Ana screams, "You sadistic bastard!"

His panting is fierce as he enjoys his sadistic attack on Ana. He slaps her hard with the palm of his hand and then quickly backswings to hit her again with the back of his hand.

Ana screams and pleads while she struggles to get away.

Jovanovic seizes the front of her blouse and rips it off.

We hear Ana as she strikes back with her fists, pounding on his bare chest. There is a struggle and the pounding stops.

Ana screams, "Let go of my wrists you pig! No, no, no."

Her skirt falls to the floor. Then we hear the ripping of nylon pantyhose. She screams, "Let me GO!" Now she is stumbling backward and falling into furniture.

Jovanovic shouts, "On your knees, bitch!"

"Ieee! Let go of my hair!"

Then there is the sound of a stick hitting the top of a table. This is followed by repeated strikes to her body, hard flesh, soft flesh and sensitive flesh.

Ana cries out, "No! Please don't... Owww ... Ahiii... Ieee... Please, stop...

His heavy breathing becomes louder and is now coupled with his sighs and groans of pleasure.

She screams in pain and we can hear her struggling to get free. Objects keep falling to the floor. Suddenly we can hear her gasping for air and choking. "Ckaaa ... No! Guuu ..."

Jovanovic whispers in a low vicious tone, "Shut up, bitch, or I'll kill you."

Then all her screams and protests become muffled as though her face were being shoved in a pillow. Her choking gives way to whimpering and sobing. "Wiii ... Huuu ... Yiaaaaaaa ..."

His guttural sounds reflect his enjoyment as he intensifies his attack.

For a moment her face is free, and she screams out, "Helllp!" But her cry becomes muffled again. She groans in pain, whimpers and sobs.

Suddenly a door is flung open and Vladimir is silhouetted in the hall light. Vladimir calls out, "Mom?!"

He flips on the light switch and stops in his tracks, frozen by the horror of what he sees in front of him. His face fills with fear, and he cannot move or speak.

Ana whimpers, "My baby?"

Jovanovic hisses, "Shut up or I'll kill the little bastard too!"

Ana calls out to Vladimir, "Run for the police!"

Vladimir turns instantly and runs out and down the hall. We can hear him taking the steps two at a time. Then there is silence.

Jovanovic says coldly, "Damn it to hell anyway!" He is quickly zipping up his trousers.

Ana says seductively, "What are you doing, Jovanovic?" She then kicks off her pantyhose.

Jovanovic looks at her, "I can't afford a confrontation with the police." He continues to get dressed, and primps in a mirror.

Ana is now angry, "You bastard! You have to finish me. You can't leave me like this. I need sex. It'll take at least a half-hour for the police to get here."

Jovanovic hisses back, "Maybe I wanted it to take longer. You should have thought of that. Besides, the kid's old enough to watch."

He looks in the mirror and straightens his tie and begins to smooth out his hair. Ana comes up behind him and tries to seduce him.

She is affectionate and playful, "Come on, baby. You know you want me. A little sex, a little pleasure, come on."

Jovanovic is not responding, "Not as bad as you do."

Suddenly, Ana explodes with anger and starts to puts on her clothes.

Ana lashes out at him, "You have a hell of a nerve coming here and getting me so turned on and then walking off and leaving me higher than a kite. I never want to see you again. Find someone else for your kinky sex. I'll get my pleasure somewhere else."

Jovanovic laughs and takes her in his arms, "You know that you can't live without me."

They kiss, and it grows more and more passionate. Then Jovanovic breaks it off and leaves her to finish getting dressed. He walks down the hall and then freezes at the head of the stairs.

Vladimir is sitting on the bottom step. His face is distorted with mental anguish and tears stream from his eyes. He doesn't move.

Jovanovic breaks into boisterous laughter and walks down the steps. As he passes Vladimir, he pats him on the head and says, "Toughen up kid. The next time I'll let you watch." He walks out laughing.

CHAPTER 7
Lies & Deceit

At the Igman arms factory, Ranko is sitting at his desk. His secretary is working a few feet away in the same office. The Security Director knocks on the open door.

The secretary looks up, "Come in."

The Security Director smiles at the secretary and glances at Ranko, "I need to talk to Ranko about an important mater."

Ranko looks up from his work, "Come on in." He does not offer him a seat.

The Security Director walks over and stands in front of Ranko's desk. He waits for Ranko to look up.

After a moment, Ranko signs the paper he is reading and holds it up for the secretary. She comes over and retrieves the paper without saying anything. Ranko studies the Security Director for a moment. At the same time, he composes himself so as not to give any clue of his personal actions.

Finally, he asks, "Well, what is so important?"

The Security Director hesitates then says timidly, "Before the other Directors find out, I thought you should know that a shipment of weapons has gone missing."

Ranko looks him in the eye, "what do you mean 'gone missing?' Are you saying they were stolen? That's pretty serious."

"I'm saying that there are several crates of weapons missing. They were moved to the shipping area on Friday and this morning they were not there."

Ranko suggests, feigning confusion, "Maybe they've been shipped."

The Security Director says, "No, I checked the bills of lading."

The phone rings, interrupting them. Ranko's secretary answers it.

"Igman Arms Factory, Director Rakic's office." She listens and then motions to Ranko. "It's the General, and it's very important." She shrugs her shoulders in apology to the Security Director.

Ranko takes the call. He is mostly listening, but the few responses that he does make sound as if he is discussing a business deal. The Security Director turns to look out the window and pretends not to be listening, but it is obvious that he is taking in every word. This is typical behavior leftover from Tito and the era of Communism. The fact that the secretary is in the same room is not for lack of space. It is the common practice so nothing can be done in secret.

Ranko is listening to a rather lengthy report from the General, "The contract is executed? They're cleansed? ...That sounds good. ...When? ...and payment? Thanks for taking care of this garbage... I'll call as soon as I finish with a problem here. ...O.K. Thanks."

Ranko hangs up. The Security Director turns back to him.

Ranko becomes very friendly toward the Security Director, projecting a sympathetic awareness to his problem, "This is terrible! Do you suspect someone of taking the shipment or could they just have been moved somewhere else?"

The Security Director welcomes Ranko's non-confrontational attitude. It means that he, personally, is not in the crosshairs. ʿMy men are checking the plant and the warehouse now, but I have my suspicions."

"Anyone I should know about?" Ranko asks coyly.

The Security Director becomes cautious, "No one specifically yet, but I have to follow up some leads."

Ranko adds, with an air of helpfulness, "This is terrible! If you come up with anything, be sure and let me know. We want to nail the bastard fast. By the way, have you checked the computer inventory list against shipments?

The Security Director's guard goes up, "Of course, I have, but they check out.

Ranko plays dumb, "Doesn't that mean they have been shipped? What makes you think they are missing?"

The Security Director becomes irritated, "I saw the crates on Friday, no shipments have been logged out the gate since then but they are gone. I don't give a damn what the computer says. Someone could be screwing with it."

Ranko changes tactics again, tries to console him and stroke his ego, "This is terrible! But as usual, you are right on top of things. I got your back on this. It's good that you brought it to my attention, and I'll look into it. Let me know if you come up with anything, but don't file a report until we are absolutely sure we know what happened to them. You know what could happen if such a report got in the wrong hands."

The Security Director relaxes, "I appreciate your backing me up on this. I knew I could count on you. Thanks."

Ranko stands and puts his hand on the Security Director's shoulder and sees him to the door. The Security Director shakes his hand and leaves.

On the way back to his desk Ranko turns to the secretary and asks, "Get my wife on the phone."

He walks to his desk and sits down. He leans back pleased with himself, lights up a cigar and pours a Jack Daniel's.

Ana picks up the phone. "Hello, Rakic residence."

The secretary responds, "Just a moment, Ana, your husband wants to talk to you." She calls to Ranko, "Ana is on line one."

He picks up the phone and presses line one. Throughout the entire conversation, he shows no emotion regardless of what his words may imply.

"Ana, I just heard from my father. We have been doing everything we could to get the store back for your mother and father in Belgrade."

"Yes, I know."

"Well, we were very near success, but last night they were both shot in their sleep."

Ana is shocked, "No!"

There is a long silence. Tears well up in Ana's eyes and roll down her cheeks. Ranko takes a sip from his glass.

Ranko continues, "I feel really bad about this." He takes a puff on his cigar. "It looks like the work of Muslim garbage. This is terrible." He takes another sip. "I'm so sorry! Honey, are you all right?"

Ranko takes another puff and sip.

Slowly Ana responds. She is all choked up, "I'm leaving for Belgrade at once."

"I'm very sorry, darling. I'll send a car to pick you up right away. As soon as you have made the arrangements for the funeral, I'll join you."

"Thank you. I'll call."

Ranko hangs up and drains his glass.

Ana hangs up. And sobs uncontrollably.

CHAPTER 8
Fairytale Device

Jusuf and Vladimir are making the strenuous climb up to Nedjo's place. Vladimir has not been able to cope with his experience at home the other night. He needed to talk to someone, so he told his best friend. Jusuf listened, but he was equally traumatized by the story. They ruled out the possibility of discussing it with Jusuf's mom and dad. This left only Nedjo, who they could trust. They make the climb in silence.

When they reach Nedjo's workshop, they knock and enter.

Jusuf calls out, "Nedjo?"

There is no answer.

They both look around for Nedjo. He is not there. Vladimir opens the door to his living area and calls up, "Nedjo! It's Vladimir and Jusuf."

There is no answer. They look at each other and shrug their shoulders. They continue to look around.

It doesn't take them long to discover two Fairytale devices on the workbench. Yes, and curiosity gets the best of them.

Vladimir says, "I don't think we should be touching these."

"Nedjo won't mind if we just look," Jusuf replies.

Jusuf puts one of the headsets on to see how it feels.

Vladimir is hesitant but asks, "What's it like?"

"It's like some sort of space odyssey."

Vladimir can't resist, so he puts on the other headset. "You're right. It's like a space ship."

Jusuf says eagerly, "Let's try them out."

Vladimir considers it for a moment, but he really wants to. He asks, "What if we can't get out of the Fairytale?"

Jusuf is overly confident, "He's solved that problem, otherwise he wouldn't have built another unit. Besides it's just a Fairytale, what can be the harm in that?"

The truth is that he built a second one, because he couldn't get the first one to work. Unfortunately, the Boys don't think of that possibility.

Vladimir is quick to agree, "That makes sense. And I could use a break. O.K., let's do it."

They plug each other into the black box.

Vladimir finds the mini diskette, "Here's the diskette marked 'Warm Fuzzies.' I'll load it."

Jusuf looks at Vladimir, "Are you ready?"

Vladimir nods yes, and Jusuf pushes the "on" button.

The device whirs into action. It sounds like a miniature computer booting up with beeps and boops. The miniature TV screens come to life and scroll with multiple colors.

Vladimir is tripping, "Ooh! This is psychedelic."

Jusuf starts to trip too, "Ah! What a trip. You can feel it through the whole body."

The pads on their temples are sending impulses into their brains as their skin twitches beneath the pads. It's going to be a wild experience for them, so hold on.

There is a flash of light and they can hear music in the head set. The background, objects, animals, birds and insects are animation as are the people. The Boys appear as puppets, which mimic their own actions. They hear a voice narrating the story.

"Once upon a time. In a very special Fairytale land, there is a secret magic, which makes it different from all other places. Because of the magic the people have a wonderful feeling of peace and harmony."

The Boys see themselves in the Fairytale scene.
They see birds flying through the air singing on tree
branches. They see butterflies flying from plant to
plant and bees humming over flowers. Many animals,
wild and domestic, roam about freely. Jusuf sees
himself feeding a deer, and it feels like he is actually
feeding the deer. Vladimir has the same experience as
he plays with a wolf. The people are moving about
the village working or doing business.

"In this small village, the people live in perfect
harmony with each other. They are of every color,
religion and ethnic variety. The Prince greets the
Farmer. The Farmer greets the Miller. The Miller
greets the Baker's Wife. The Baker's Wife greets the
Merchant. The Merchant greets the Carpenter. The
Carpenter greets the Farmer's Wife. The Farmer's
Wife greets the Prince. A greeting is a smile, a wave, a
joyful word, a cheerful hello, or a kind and friendly
word and sometimes all of the above."

The Boys are watching
them pass and greet each other.
Then just as Vladimir and Jusuf
are greeting each other, the voice
says, "And the 'Fair-haired Child'
greets the 'Dark-haired Child'."

Vladimir and Jusuf look
at each other with a puzzling expression on their faces,
because Vladimir has blond hair and Jusuf has black
hair. They both look around wondering how the
narrator could possibly know that.

"The people are of every size, shape and appearance. They are noble folk, merchants, tradesman and farmers, but all are free people. All are equal, men and women alike. Even, the animals share in the harmony, cats and dogs alike.

"The 'Dark-haired Child' and the 'Fair-haired Child' stop to watch a dog and cat as they are playing with each other. The dog lies down. The cat licks his face. The children play with them and pet them."

As this happens, Jusuf and Vladimir are part of the action now. They are not just seeing it and experiencing it, they are immersed into it.

"It is a joyful land smiling with flowers and sunshine. They are a joyful people who glow with love and kindness. In the spring new life and joy fills the air. When gray clouds bring April showers to the land, everything drinks deep and the rivers sing with joy. The flowers bloom. The bees  make honey. The pastures turn green again. Farmers plow and plant the fields, and everything starts to grow. All is well!

"With summer comes the smiling sun and cooling showers. The children play and laugh. The people do the summer work cheerfully. The gardens produce food in abundance for everyone. The crops grow and ripen. All is well!

"Autumn brings the beautiful colors. The crops yield their harvest to sell or store. All hands work to make it so. All hands share the bounty of their labors. All hearts are greatly thankful. A storm blows down a barn, and the next day all the people come and put it up again. All is well!

"Festive lights dispel the darkness of winter. The cold is warmed by friendly hearths. So the sun is always in their hearts and the light fills their faces. 'Tis the season of joyful song and celebration of their blessings. All is well! All is well! All is well!

"What is the magic that makes this possible? If you look closely at all the people young or old, you will see a leather bag hanging from each person's waist. The bags are round and plump.

"Watch as it happens. The Boys interact with the people sharing their 'warm fuzzies' with them and each other. As people take 'warm fuzzies' from their bags, a glitter floats through the air and the bags shrink. All the 'warm fuzzies' are given away until the bag is empty. But when the cock crows at firstlight, the bags pop full again.

"Where do they get these bags? You can see each man, woman and child has a bag of 'warm fuzzies.' Well, when a love baby is born a bag appears in the cradle beside it, which is stuffed full of 'warm fuzzies.' But you must remember, the tradition is that you must give away all your 'warm fuzzies,' and every time the bag is empty – by cock's first crow at dawn the bag becomes full again.

"Each time a kindness is offered or a loving word is spoken a 'warm fuzzy' sparkles from their bags and touches the heart of the other person.

"This is how it works. When the Prince is out riding trough the fields and comes upon a Farmer plowing the land, he goes out of his way to greet him and give him a 'warm fuzzy.'

"The Prince says, 'What fine straight furrows you plow!'

"The Farmer replies, 'What a fine braid you set in your steed's mane.'

"That is the way it goes the whole day long. When the Farmer takes his grain to the Miller...

"The Farmer says, 'Take your time, your fine flour is worth waiting for.'

"When the Miller says good night to the Carpenter, who is repairing his roof...

"The Miller says, 'Thank you for a good day's work. Give my best to your fine wife.'

"The Carpenter replies, 'Thank you for the work, and the best to your wife as well.'

"They never count the 'warm fuzzies' they gave away, or what is left in their bags. The only time a cross word is ever spoken is when someone runs out of 'warm fuzzies' before noon. However, all is made right the next morning, for the bag is always full again.

"Then one day, a Wicked Witch flies over the happy land and swoops down into the village. She becomes invisible and looks around the village. She is very angry at what she finds there as she meets the people along the road.

"First, she meets the 'Fair-haired Child' and the 'Dark-haired Child' playing with a ball in the village street. One falls down and the other helps him to get up, and a 'warm fuzzy' is given.

"Then she sees a man drop his bundle and a woman stoops to help him put it together again, and gives him a 'warm fuzzy'.

"The Wicked Witch screams, 'Why, these people are so good it makes me ill!'"

At this point in the story, Jusuf lifts the control box to the Fairytale device and presses the "stop" button. The lights flash, but the Fairytale continues for a moment longer. He repeats this three times while the action continues.

"The Wicked Witch overhears a discussion between two people, who agreed and end up sharing 'warm fuzzies'

 "The Wicked Witch is very angry, 'Don't they know that a good argument never hurts anybody?'

"The Wicked Witch's anger is like a violent thunderstorm. The rain pounds down in large droplets and the Boys are getting soaked. The lightning strikes and dances around them."

At this point, the Boys take off their headsets. The Fairytale stops and all the video disappears. The Boys stand and look at each other, then feel themselves all over. They are dry. They are both so excited that they start to talk at once.

Jusuf says, "What an incredible trip!"

Vladimir says, "It felt just like we were there!"

"The Wicked Witch was so real!"

"So scary! Did you see me? I could see you!"

"Yes! It's incredible!"

"Fantastic! Let's do it again! I can't wait to see how it comes out."

Jusuf exclaims, "Nedjo has solved the problem."

Vladimir trying to be optimistic, "It sure looks that way."

Jusuf adds cautiously, "We'll have to come back and finish the Fairytale when he's here."

CHAPTER 9
The Election

By November, the new republic of Bosnia-Herzegovina is holding its first election. We are attending the late night victory celebration in Sarajevo for the Serbian Party. Along with all the others, who worked so hard on the campaign, we are anxiously awaiting the returns. The hall is all abuzz with shoo-in victory talk. The subject of loss is unthinkable. The reporters from the TV station are milling about conducting interviews. The party leaders are also working the floor. The candidates are not there yet.

With a great fanfare from the band, a party leader comes onto the platform and tries to get the crowd's attention. This takes several minutes as the crowd cheers and chants different victory slogans.

Finally, the crowd settles down a little and the leader shouts into the mic, "Ladies and gentleman, I give you Djoric, our Serbian candidate for the Konjic district."

He comes out onto the platform and the crowd erupts again in cheers and applause. Djoric tries to settle them down repeatedly. He is all smiles and bubbling with joy as he makes his feeble attempts to quiet them.

After a few minutes, the crowd calms down enough for Djoric to try to speak over their shouts. "The early estimates, from the Serbian voting places, give us an overwhelming majority."

The crowd erupts again and the band goes wild. People are hugging each other and jumping up and down. Djoric struggles to get their attention. He says into the mic, "That's the good news." But no one can hear him. He motions for them to settle down, but the people pay no attention to him. He repeats over and over again, "That's only the good news." It takes over a dozen attempts before the crowed starts to pick-up on his less than enthusiastic attitude, and they start to quiet down.

Djoric finally shouts over the crowd, "However... However... However, we haven't been able to get any accurate numbers from the other polling places. But we have every reason to be optimistic. Maybe if we call him loud enough, we can get the General to come out and say a few words before the results are in."

The crowd starts to chant, "Rakic, Rakic, Rakic, Rakic, Rakic..." Everyone's eyes are glued to the platform entrance and eagerly awaiting the General's arrival.

Suddenly the double doors in the back of the hall are flung open. Two security guards step in and to the side of the door. General Rakic steps in holding up his arm and hand with his fingers forming the victory sign. The crowd goes wild. The General starts to work the crowd "pressing the flesh." Ranko, Ana and Jovanovic follow him in. Jovanovic and Ranko join in the greeting of the people in the crowd. Ana clings to Ranko's arm.

The General is charming and friendly. Improvising, he thanks those he greets for their help and support. Many of them give the General a quick

Serbian three-finger salute and say, "Long live the Greater Serbia!"

Ranko is also enjoying the "pressing of the flesh." Ana smiles and laughs. She is trying to look supportive of her man. However, there is a subtle stiffness and artificiality in her actions. Jovanovic looks on ogling Ana. His perverted thoughts do not reveal any recognition of her falseness. However, his face and body language reveal his perverted desires and pure lust.

Slowly they work their way toward the stage. Finally, they mount the stage and the General struggles to bring the audience to order until he can finally speak. After a few minutes, he speaks enthusiastically.

"... Thank you. ... Thank you. ....You are too kind. ....Thank you." He holds up his hand for silence, and the crowd quickly becomes quiet. "I can't begin to tell you how much your hard work and enthusiastic support have meant to me personally. It is I who should applaud you for your effort." He applauds them.

"Tonight is an historical occasion for the people of Bosnia-Herzegovina. Tonight we shall witness the birth of our new republic, and tonight we shall take our place as the leaders of that republic."

The crowd applauds and cheers. He smiles and enjoys the moment. After a few moments, he holds up his hand for silence again.

Rakic continues, "Throughout the history of Yugoslavia, the Serbian people have always been the natural leaders. They have always held the positions of responsibility. They have been the keepers of the peace, the protectors of law and order. Can there be any question as to who should lead this new republic into the future?"

A wild applause erupts. After a moment, he motions for silence.

Rakic is becoming more and more powerful, "The future shall be ours! We shall make Bosnia-Herzegovina a prosperous and productive republic. We shall make the farms the model for all of Eastern Europe, with modern technology and sound business management. We shall build our industrial strength to compete with the rest of the world. The future is ours, and tonight we seize our destiny."

The crowd goes wild stomping their feet and applauding. After a moment, he signals for silence and they obey his command.

Rakic is on a roll and pushes the tempo to the top, "Ever since I was a young man, I had the dream of a strong federation of Serbian States. Tonight Bosnia-Herzegovina shall take its place as the second state in that federation. I have spoken to Milosevic and he shares this dream. Tomorrow shall be the birth of a Serbian union, so that every Serb, no matter what land he may live in, shall be first and foremost a citizen of the Greater Serbia. This is our birthright. Lift up your heads. Walk tall and proud! We are Serbian! Long live the Serbian ideal!" His hand shoots up with the three-finger salute.

The crowd explodes wildly with their hands shooting up in the three-finger salute. A chant begins. "Serbia! Serbia! Serbia!" The crowd is almost out of control. Rakic relishes in the reaction.

A very solemn messenger enters from the stage door walks over to Djoric and hands him a piece of paper. He reads it to himself and then motions for Rakic to come to one side. A smiling and laughing Rakic swaggers over to him. Rakic reads the note, and his countenance falls immediately. He looks up at Djoric not knowing what to do. Djoric puts a comforting hand on his shoulder for a moment and then walks up to podium. The crowed, who sees this, becomes dead silent in an instant.

Djoric holds up the paper and begins in a very somber tone, "I have the results." He looks at the note and begins to read. "The Muslim party has won with 57% of the vote."

Rakic, who is looking at the floor, is shaking his head in shock.

"The Croatian party has 24%, the Socialists have 13% and the Serbian party is last with only 6% of the vote."

Rakic explodes with growing anger, shouting, "They can't do this to us!"

Djoric rushes through the rest of the message, "All the local contests including Sarajevo and Konjic are mixed between the Muslims, Croatians and Socialists. The Serbs are completely out, right straight across the board."

The crowd becomes very still for a moment.

Rakic charges to the podium and shoves Djoric aside. Enraged, he shouts into the microphone, "We are Serbian! Serbs are winners! If a Serb has a piece of garbage in his kitchen, he throws it out to fertilize the soil. So let's get rid of the garbage. Let's get rid of the heathen Muslims and Catholic Croatians once and for all."

Djoric realizes that they are being broadcast on TV and tries to cover for Rakic. He moves back to the podium and motions for the TV cameras to cut.

Djoric says calmly, "Ladies and gentleman, people of Bosnia-Herzegovina, the results are in. Unfortunately, we have lost at every level in this race. We will now cut to the studio where we can post the results for you."

The cameras cut, and the large screen on the back of the stage goes blank for a moment. A violent "BOO" goes up from the crowd, with shouts of outrage. Suddenly, the cameras pop back on and everyone can see the picture on the screen as it pans the crowd. Rakic pushes his way back to the podium.

Rakic is now out of control, "I declare this election null and void. The Serbs will decide who will be the president! WE are the *master race*! It is time to bear arms and take what is rightfully ours. It is time to cleanse the land…"

Ranko and Jovanovic take hold of Rakic and try to get him off the platform.

As they drag him off, Rakic continues shouting in a rage, "We shall drive them out, or their blood and rotting bodies shall fertilize the soil!"

The crowd cheers Rakic and shoots their arms up in the three-finger salute. They are frantically out of control.

Ranko, Jovanovic and Rakic disappear through the stage door. Djoric follows. The crowd chants hateful slogans!

Ana stands alone on the platform for a moment, with a terrified expression on her face. The camera zooms in on her to capture the moment. She then slowly backs out of the stage door.

The crowd continues to jeer and shout threats.

CHAPTER 10
Soccer

For a while, life goes on as usual in Konjic. Jusuf and Nedjo are attending a soccer match in which Vladimir is one of the star players.

Vladimir is moving the ball down the field. He is a natural at this game, and his moves are almost magical. Vladimir drives in close to the goal, he passes off, moves into position and the ball is passed back to him. He scores. The crowd cheers wildly.

Jusuf and Nedjo cheer from their seats in the bleachers.

It is now three weeks since the elections and we are in the middle of the soccer playoffs. So far, all is well, but there is a noticeable tension in the air.

Nedjo is wearing an optical device, which gives him perfect vision. It looks like a plastic headband that goes over the eyes with a group of honeycomb cells in front. At the right temple is a miniature TV camera, about the size of a matchbox. At the left temple is a small range finder. The headband connects to a control box about the size of a deck of cards, which he has in his pocket.

Jusuf asks, "How's it working?"

Nedjo is excited, "Fantastic! It's just like I am there."

Jusuf laughs, "You are there."

Nedjo laughs as well, "Of course I am."

We hear a voice over a loudspeaker, "The ball is put back in play again. It moves down the field and is passed to Vladimir... But wait a minute, he is standing there frozen in his tracks. The ball bounces off his belly and falls to the ground in front of him. What's going on here? The other players move in to take the ball and Vladimir is knocked to the ground."

Vladimir falls to the turf.

Jusuf moves blindly out of the stands and onto the field. He makes his way to Vladimir.

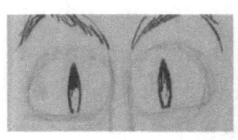 From the boy's perspective, there are flashing lights and they start to go into the Fairytale.

Nedjo gets up and tries to move to the field.

We too slide into the Fairytale. We can hear the announcer over the loud speaker, "Ladies and gentlemen, there is chaos on the playing field. One of the students is wandering out to Vladimir. What are they doing? Please keep your seats!"

The Wicked Witch swoops into the Fairytale village. The Dark-Haired Child and the Fair-Haired Child start to play with an imaginary ball.

The announcer says, "It looks like they are playing with an imaginary ball!"

The Wicked Witch is watching the Fair-haired Child playing ball with the Dark-haired Child. She says, "After all, it is a great thing to see that you are different from your neighbor and know that you are better."

The Boys laugh and play, congratulating each other and share their 'warm fuzzies.' We can see them sparkle out of their bags and into the heart of their friend.

The Fair-haired Child (Vladimir) says, "Good kick!"

The Dark-haired Child (Jusuf) responds, "Great move, champ."

Suddenly, the Boys freeze.

We hear the announcer over the speaker, "Now they seem to be frozen in their tracks. In all my years, I have never seen anything like this.

In the Fairytale, the Wicked Witch screeches in disgust.

The People who agreed come walking down the road, and the man and woman with the dropped bundle are standing by the brook.

The Wicked Witch begins to spin around waving her arms in the air creating a small tornado that zooms up the road. First, the tornado blows the Fair-haired Child's ball into a tar pot, then it blows dirt in the mouths of the two people who agreed, and finally it blows the bread into the brook, which the man has dropped from his bundle.

From the soccer field, we hear the sound of a referee whistle blowing frantically. Then we hear the voice of the announcer, "The referees are trying to bring order to the playing field.

"The coach is moving onto the playing field. He doesn't look happy. He is working his way to Vladimir and the other boy, who they tell me is Jusuf. The coach is shaking his fist at Vladimir.

We can hear the voice of the coach over the speaker, "You stupid, clumsy bastard! You'll never play in the Olympics! You're finished!"

The announcer says, "Now Nedjo is on the field and moving toward the coach. Nedjo is trying to intervene."

Through the following, the Fairytale and the action surrounding the soccer game occur simultaneously.

The Wicked Witch laughs hysterically, but then the two boys look at the ball, and the Dark-haired Child offers his own.

The Dark-haired Child says, "We can use mine to make a tar-baby."

They kneel down over the tar pot and start to build a tar-baby. They laugh and thoroughly enjoy getting their hands in the messy tar.

Nedjo says to the coach, "Don't be angry! Can't you see something's wrong?"

The coach pushes him out of the way, "Get the hell out'a my way!"

He knocks Nedjo down, and crushes the control box in the confusion.

Nedjo is blind again. "Beelzebub! Now look at what you've done. You broke it."

The coach shouts, "Big deal! I broke your walkman."

"You broke my new vision set. I'm blind again."

Coach flips him off, "You've always been blind." Then he screams at the Boys, "What the hell are they doing now? Playing patty cake!"

The announcer's voice comes over the speaker again, "The coach is very angry. He is trying to get to Vladimir. What is the Gypsy doing out there? Wait a minute the Boys are kneeling down playing with something."

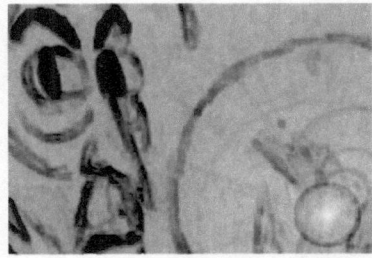 Meanwhile in the Fairytale, after the dirt blew in the mouths of the two people who agree, they started sputtering and spitting, but they naturally offer each other their handkerchiefs.

Suddenly the coach realizes what he has done and helps Nedjo to his feet. He apologizes, "I'm sorry for the broken box."

Nedjo says, "I'm not concerned about that. I can build a new one. But, I am concerned about The Boys. Can you take me to them?"

"Of course!" The coach takes his arm and leads him toward The Boys.

Finally, in the Fairytale, the woman who is helping the man pick up his bundle, scoops the bread from the brook and offers the Man her own instead. She says, "You must take mine. For I am going to make bread pudding, and you will save me the soaking."

The Wicked Witch begins to tear out her hair and scream. "I must find a way to end this 'warm fuzzy' business, this helping business, this kindly business, this friendly business, this gushy business. Yuuuuuuuuk!"

She screeches with such a soul-piercing sound that it brings Vladimir and Jusuf out of the Fairytale. She and the other Fairytale people disappear from our view. Once again, the Fairytale vanishes, and we too are free from it, at least for the moment.

Jusuf and Vladimir are still kneeling on the soccer field. They look at each other in total amazement. Confusion is written all over their faces. They each pinch themselves to test the reality of the present situation.

Vladimir asks Jusuf, "What is going on?"

Nedjo is just now reaching them. He says, "That was my exact question."

They look up at him and blurt out what they have done. They are frightened.

"We tried the Fairytale devices. We thought you fixed it," Jusuf confesses.

Vladimir explains, "The Fairytale started all by itself without the headset."

Nedjo is shocked, "Oh, the hell you say!"

"I'll give you fairy tale!" The coach is very confused. "You want to tell me what the hell is going on?"

Nedjo pretends confidence, "It's O.K. It's O.K. I'll get you out. I don't know how just now, but I'll get you out. Don't worry; I'll take care of it, coach.

The loudspeaker comes on again with the announcer's voice, "May I have your attention, please? May I have your attention, please! I am sorry to announce that General Rakic has been assassinated in Sarajevo. It is believed to be the work of Muslim extremists. We are canceling and rescheduling the game in respect for this great leader of the Bosnia-Herzegovinian people."

Nedjo mumbles to himself, "Oh NO, now it starts again."

CHAPTER 11
Unholy Night

Meho and Jusuf are working in the cabinet shop. They are doing a thorough cleaning from top to bottom. Every piece of machinery has been cleaned out and dusted off. Every shelf has been emptied, cleaned, the contents vacuumed and neatly rearranged on the shelf. Jusuf is now sweeping the floor, and Meho is cleaning the windows. The whole place is starting to sparkle.

It is Christmas Eve. Most Muslims in Bosnia celebrate this holiday in honor of their Catholic and Orthodox friends. Meho and Jusuf are singing Christmas carols as they work.

Meho turns to Jusuf and asks, "What did you get your mom this year?"

Jusuf stops singing and walks over to his backpack, which is hanging up. He takes a package out of the backpack. The wrapping paper is very fine and tied with silver garland. He carefully unties the garland and unfolds the wrapping paper. He holds up the box for his father to see and admire, "I saved up and bought her a new hairbrush."

Meho is astonished, "Oh, I know she'll love that."

Jusuf puts the hairbrush back in the box and meticulously rewraps it. He turns to his father, "What have you done?"

Meho walks over to the corner of the shop. He takes something up with a cloth wrapped around it. Proudly he removes the cloth to reveal a beautiful hand-carved bookstand. "I carved this for her, to hold her cook book."

Jusuf walks over to admire it, "Wow that sure is…"

Without warning, the lights flash in Jusuf's mind. He begins to see the Fairytale. Vladimir is already there. Both of them go into a Fairytale trance, each in the place where they are at that moment.

Meho is concerned, "Jusuf? What's the matter? Jusuf. Jusuf!"

The Wicked Witch swoops into the village. She spins around mumbling an enchantment and turns herself into a milkmaid. Every part of her appears to be a collection of different pieces from a dozen different fairy tale milkmaids. Her bonnet, with her hair

tucked up into it, has six bows tied under her chin. Her face is round with a tiny nose and rosy dimpled cheeks. Her dress is plain and straight, but about two sizes too small for her body. Her sleeves cover her

arms and taper at the wrist. Her hands are large and
strong with very long fingers. Her feet are bare, large
and healthy looking. Yet she has the tiniest toes you
ever did see.

She dances about with a wooden milk bucket
and finally sits outside the Prince's castle. There she
poses on her plump-plump and begins to cry in her
milk bucket.

When the
Prince comes out
for his morning
ride, he sees the
milkmaid. For she
is pretty hard to
miss, after all.

Prince says
politely, "What is the matter my beautiful maid?"

Here it is important to point out that he
actually means it, for a 'warm fuzzy' comes sparkling
from his bag and bounces around her heart.

The milkmaid shakes it off, "Boohoo.
Boohoo! It is terrible, my lord! Yesterday by three, I
had given all my 'fuzzies' away, and this morning my
bag was not filled. Has the magic left the village?
Boohoo, atchoo!"

The Prince says kindly, "Don't fear, my child!
You shall have half of mine."

With that, he reaches in his bag and gives her
about half of all he has. He smiles, tips his hat and
rides away.

As soon as he is out of sight, the Wicked
Witch spits on the 'warm fuzzies,' throws them to the

ground and tramples them into the dust with her large round feet and tiny toes.

She then flies on ahead. When she lands, she does a rolling summersault while saying an enchantment. As she stands up, she turns into a potbellied holy man. He is wearing a monk's robe and sandals. His hair is long and knotted, with a bald spot shaved on the crown of his head. With difficulty, he pulls his robe down around his waist, so he is naked from the waist up. He sits down on a large stone alongside the road and begins to beat himself on the back with a birch branch. "Ouch! That feels good. Yikes! That's wonderful. Argh, ow, yeow! I'm in heaven."

Soon the Prince rides down the road and passes the holy man. He stops and flinches at the holy man's pain, "What is the matter, good Father? Why do you punish yourself so?"

The holy man pretends to be in pain and suffering, "I am a wicked and sinful man. I do not deserve the love of any man, for God is punishing me. Every day I give all my 'fuzzies' away, but this morning my bag was left empty. Why has the magic deserted me? I pray it has not abandoned anyone else?"

The Prince is puzzled, "Why, in fact it has. This morning I have met one other whose bag was not filled. I gave her about half of what I had in my bag."

The holy man writhes in pretended agony, "Oh God, why? WHY?! We must repent of our wicked ways if we are to be saved! I fear the magic has left this village. Please my lord; can you spare me half of what is in your bag?

For the first time in the Prince's life, he hesitates. It is very unusual for anyone to counts the number of 'warm fuzzies' in their bag. But the Prince starts counting. "Let me see. …oh my. …that can't be. …this will not do. ..If I give you half, I shall have only *six* left!

The holy man holds out his hand begging, "But six will make me so very happy, and God will be pleased with your generosity."

The Prince says reluctantly, "Very well, you shall have half." With that, he carefully counts out six 'fuzzies' one at a time. His countenance changes as he rides on, with his head down.

The Wicked Witch takes the 'fuzzies,' spits on them and throws them into the dung that the horse leaves behind. She then flies on ahead, bounces off a thatch roof and lands on the front porch of a cottage.

 She waves her arms in four directions then up and down while saying an enchantment. She then snaps the fingers on both hands and turns herself into an old

widow woman. She has a large nose with a wart on it and very bushy eyebrows. Her cheeks are over powdered with very red rouge. Her apron and bonnet are badly soiled. Her dress is made of many parts of once fine garments and sewn poorly together in a tasteless way. Her shoes are badly worn and of two different colors, two different sizes and two different styles.

As the Prince rides into the village square, He sees the widow woman, who is pounding on the door to her house and screaming in anger.

The widow woman screeches out, "Open this door, you wicked children!"

The Prince snaps at her in a very unfriendly

manner, "Woman, hold your tongue! You'll disturb the peace and alarm the village."

But she continues to rant and rave. She looks over her shoulder then turns back to the door concealing an evil smirk. She screeches in a shrill tone that hurts the ears, "You wicked children! I'm going to beat you within an inch of your life!"

This is so unusual; the folk begin to come out to see what is happening. Soon the village square is full of people. They have never seen anything like this. Then the talking begins, buzz, buzz, buzz. The Wicked Witch is really enjoying this.

The widow woman pounds and screeches, "You rotten children. Open this door at once! I am your mother, and you owe me some respect!"

The Prince is furious, "Shut up, woman! Or I shall have you put away."

The widow woman starts to move among the crowd. She explains in a condemning tone, "My son and his wife woke up this morning and their bags were not filled. When I looked in my bag it was left empty as well. I was so frightened that I dropped a pitcher of milk. My son and daughter-in-law were so angry at me they threw me out of the house. What am I to do? The magic has left the village." She turns back to the Prince. "Can you spare me just one 'fuzzy'?

A darkness comes into the Prince's face. He puts on a royal air and says, "This morning I have met two others who awoke to find their bags unfilled. I shared with each about half of all I had left in my bag.

I now have only six left." He turns to the crowd around him. "Is there anyone here that will test the magic of the village and give this woman a 'fuzzy'?"

For the first time ever, one by one the townsfolk begin to count their 'warm fuzzies'.

The widow woman rushes among them begging, "Is there no one who will help me? Just one small 'fuzzy'!"

Slowly the villagers turn their backs on her and walk away. Only Jusuf who is now the Carpenter and Vladimir who is now the Prince remain.

The widow woman screeches with an evil grin, "You're all hypocrites! Now I see who you really are! You're pious snobs, rotten do-gooders!"

Jusuf and Vladimir are both transfixed.

As the widow woman bounces down the road, she turns back into the Wicked Witch.

When she stands up, she is laughing to herself. Slowly the laughter builds into an evil screech, and she flies away.

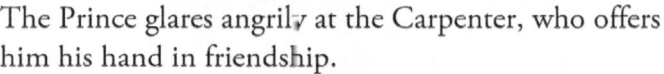

Meho is standing over Jusuf. Jusuf doesn't move.

The Fairytale traps Vladimir and Jusuf in the story. The Prince glares angrily at the Carpenter, who offers him his hand in friendship.

Ranko comes barging through the door. He is dressed in militia fatigues and carrying an automatic weapon. He steps in front of Vladimir and watches Meho.

Meho shakes Jusuf, "Jusuf, snap out of it. What's wrong with you?

Ranko shouts, "Meho! You were part of the plot against the General. You killed him."

Meho is startled and turns quickly. He sees Ranko and smiles. He says in a friendly tone, "Don't be silly, I'm not political. I know the importance of family. Come, sit down. We can talk. You have my sympathy. It must be hard for you."

The Prince walks up to the Carpenter face to face. There is anger and rage in the Prince's eyes. He shouts, "You're a liar and a traitor.

The Carpenter pleads, "Please, my lord, I have done nothing wrong. I am thy faithful servant."

Ranko shouts, "You lie! You heathen garbage!"

Meho responds calmly, "Ranko, I have known you for years. Why would I lie to you? Come, let us be friends.

In an irrational flash, the Prince draws his sword and cuts off the Carpenter's head. The lights flash in the Boys' eyes and they both come out of the Fairytale.

Vladimir and Jusuf are both standing in the middle of the cabinet shop. Vladimir looks around puzzled as to how he got there. Then he looks at Jusuf, who is equally puzzled as to what happened.

Jusuf shakes off the Fairytale and the image of himself as the Carpenter and steps over to the end of the workbench.

Vladimir is finding it difficult to shake off what he just did in the Fairytale. He looks at Jusuf with fear and regret in his eyes, as he backs away.

Ranko screams, "I could never be friends with garbage like you!" He opens fire with his automatic weapon and guns him down.

Meho's bullet-riddled body flies backwards across the shop. It smashes into the finishing solvents, which crash to the floor. Ranko marches over and lights them with a match. The solvents explode engulfing the shop in flames. The flames pull back for a second then dance violently across the floor.

The Boys are frozen where they stand. Their faces twist and contort with the witnessed violence.

Ranko grabs Vladimir by the arm and pulls him out the shop door.

Aisha rushes in from the house and sees Jusuf frozen in place. She pulls him out the front door.

The fire sucks in air and then the old dry timbers seem to explode all at once. In an instant, the flames are dancing out of control through the whole house.

Aisha looks back and screams, "MEHO!"

CHAPTER 12
Think Positive

It is Christmas morning and Nedjo has worked through the night to solve the problem with the Fairytale device. He is now sound asleep at his workbench and wearing the headset.

Jusuf comes in and stands in the doorway for a moment. He studies Nedjo carefully before approaching him. After a few minutes, he walks over and gently shakes him. Nedjo wakes up slowly and stretches.

Jusuf waits until he is fully awake before asking, "I came to ask if you would come to papa's funeral and say some words.

Nedjo puts a comforting hand on his shoulder, "I would be honored."

"Good, it will be just before sunset. I'm sorry to have bothered you."

Jusuf turns to leave. It is painfully obvious that the boy is deeply distressed.

Nedjo tries to comfort him, "I'm sorry, Jusuf. This is an awful thing to have to go through."

Jusuf bursts into tears, "It's too much. Why is this happening to me? I have done nothing wrong. Is it the Fairytale that is making it happen?"

"The Fairytale only presents a universal theme, which seems to parallel your situation. If a hundred people around the world were to be in the Fairytale, they would each see a parallel to their own lives. I worked all night to fix the problem. Come, let's try something."

"I'll try anything," Jusuf says anxiously.

Nedjo studies the device on the bench, "I need an NEC D1815G chip from an old calculator." He starts going through old calculators. "There are two paths in life, and that gives us the freedom of three choices. We can chose the path of darkness and live with power, greed and corruption, or we can chose the path of light and live with love and kindness. Here it is!"

He finds the chip he is looking for, and he takes the old calculator to his bench and removes the chip. He then removes something from the Fairytale device and solders in the new chip.

Nedjo continues, "Each path has its own energy, and the one with the most people is always the strongest. Today that would be the dark path. I think it was Mohammed that said, 'the demons reward you with a gold coin for every foul deed, but in hell, they place them on the spirit and heat them white hot for all eternity.'

"There let's try it again." He presses the buttons and nothing happens.

Jusuf's disappointment shows, "What's wrong? Is it going to work?"

Nedjo puts the headset on Jusuf and fiddles with the inside circuit board... "Think positive thoughts, Jusuf. To choose the path of light you must find the strength in yourself. You learn that love is not love until it is given away; kindness is only kindness when it expects nothing in return. The goal is to end up with nothing, and having done that you suddenly discover that you have everything."

He presses the buttons, but nothing happens.

"I'm thinking positive." Jusuf says quickly.

Nedjo is still fiddling, "That's odd. Let's check this here."

Nedjo plugs the box into his computer and then starts to punch in commands.

"I know you can make it work."

"There it is. We have an error with the automatic backup.

Nedjo's fingers race on the keyboard, as he works out the problem. His special Braille screen fills with computer language and scrolls up.

Jusuf reflects, "You said there were three choices."

"Oh, yes, the third choice. That is to take neither path, to pledge allegiance to the demons of neutrality."

Jusuf reacts, "Demons of neutrality? To do nothing is wrong?"

Nedjo explains, "In a healthy family a child is taught the difference between right and wrong. But when you grow up, some will try to convince you that nothing is black or white. Thus, your attention is misdirected from what is right or wrong, and you live your life in the gray zone, the zone of 'not really bad' and 'kind of good'."

"What is our demon then?"

"We all have two voices, a demon and a guardian angel. The demon is always louder, and very clever. Look, I'll give you a moral choice. You tell me what you would do, and I'll tell you what your demon and angel are saying to you."

"Sounds good," Jusuf can't wait. "O.K. What's the moral choice?"

"You see a woman drop something valuable in the street and go into her house. The street sweeper is coming down the hill and will soon sweep it up. What would you do?"

Jusuf considers, "I would pick it up..." He pauses. "...and return it to the woman."

"Your demon said to you that you should keep it, because the woman would think it got swept away."

"What are you doing, reading my mind?"

"No, I only hear the voices of your demon or your angel."

"But it was like a thought that popped into my head. Was it my demon that said that?"

"Yes, and then your angel said it didn't belong to you. But the demon said the woman would never know. So you hesitated, and if you had not made a choice it would have been swept away and lost forever."

Jusuf considers it, "Then the demon would have won!"

Nedjo smiles and responds, "Exactly, if they can't win you to the path of darkness, they can at least neutralize you so you can cause them no harm."

Suddenly one command starts to appear on the computer screen and repeats over and over.

Nedjo reacts, "Oh no. The program is in a glitch." All his attempts to stop it fail. "I have to reboot and start all over. Were you thinking positive?"

"I'm thinking about your example."

"That's thinking positive."

The corners of Jusuf's mouth turn up into a small smile. Soon Nedjo's fingers are dancing on the keys again.

Jusuf is pondering the example, "But most people are neutral, and they think that's good."

"Yes, like many governments. However, the prophecy is that when one out of every 100 people has chosen the path of light, then all those who have been neutralized shall become a flood of humanity on the path of light. Only then will the world change." Nedjo punches a couple more keys. "O.K. Got it! Let's try it again."

He turns it on, and it shorts out. Sparks and smoke rise from the circuit board. A shock shoots through the headset, and Jusuf pulls it off quickly.

Jusuf's optimism sinks, "I've had enough for one day, but I like your story."

Nedjo tries not to show his disappointment and bewilderment with the problem. "You must remember, Jusuf, that those who walk the path of light discover that their darkest moments bring them their brightest visions."

Jusuf ponders that for a moment, "I'm not sure that I understand, but I promise not to hate Vladimir. Maybe he will come to the funeral and we can patch things up."

They say their goodbyes and Jusuf heads to his shelter in the old laundry room under their burned-out house.

CHAPTER 13
An Islamic Funeral

There are heavy dark clouds in the cold winter sky. A small group of male friends have gathered at the cemetery for Meho's burial. The Imam reads from the Qur'an and speaks over the grave. Jusuf and Nedjo stand together. Nedjo is wearing his vision device.

As the Imam reads, they lower the coffin into the ground. Jusuf keeps looking for Vladimir, but he doesn't come.

The Imam reads, "Only prudent persons bear the covenant, those who fulfill God's agreement and do not break the covenant, ...they will have the compensation of the final Home, gardens of Eden which they will enter, as well as anyone who has acted honorably among their forefathers, their spouses and their offspring. Angels will come in on them by every gate: 'Peace be upon you because you have acted so patiently!' How blissful will the compensation of the Home be!"

Jusuf whispers to Nedjo while the Imam reads, "Nedjo, can you zoom in on that boy out there? Is it Vladimir?"

Nedjo looks off to the other side of the cemetery and adjusts his head set. He whispers, "It's the gravedigger."

Jusuf is disappointed and hangs his head. When the Imam finishes with his reading, Nedjo steps forward and starts to speak over Meho.

"Meho was a man of peace and love. Yet his life was taken by a dark spirit that moves among us. Unless we fight back these demons and bolster up the light in our hearts, there shall be a flood of killing far worse than our minds can..."

As Jusuf listens intently to Nedjo's words, the lights flash in his mind, and Jusuf finds himself unwillingly sliding into the Fairytale. Nedjo's voice

begins to fade into the background no matter how much he fights it off. The Fairytale people start to appear. The funeral party becomes more and more distant. Jusuf watches the Fairytale people as though he were there.

Back in the Fairytale kingdom, the rumor soon spreads throughout the village and over the land that the magic is gone and the bags will never be filled again. Ever so slowly a darkness creeps in upon the land and works its way into the heart of every man, woman and child.

Everything is changed. In the spring, the dark clouds bring very little rain. The poisonous spraying for insects leaves the ground covered with dead bees and their little legs sticking up in the air. Very little is growing and much, which does, is not pollinated.

The summer sun is scorching hot and people have very little to eat or drink.

The autumn produces only a small harvest and the poor begin to starve. Autumn storms blow down barns that no one wants to rebuild.

The winter is harsh and the snow deep. It truly becomes the season of death and death becomes the end of all things rather than the beginning.

Mothers have children without love and they are born without bags of 'warm fuzzies' in their cribs. The parents explain that even though they don't give them any of their 'warm fuzzies' they still care for them and are trying to prepare them for life.

Packs of children run through the streets destroying everything in sight.

Neighbors stop trusting each other and soon speak very little. They do business together, but only to make money. The new rule is that the more money you have the more important you are and the more power you have over others.

The village breaks apart. All the fine homes move to one area and the poorer homes to another area. The same thing happens to the churches, then finally to the people.

People begin to see that they are different and the village divides itself by class and kind. The Bres hate the Civals. The Etiw look down on the Calb. Every church claims to be right and all others they believe are wrong, until the people don't know what to believe or do not believe in anything.

As Jusuf fights the horror of what he sees, the lights flash in his mind's eye; the Fairytale and its people start to fade out. Jusuf looks to Nedjo, who does a double take, realizing what he just went through. He then continues.

"...but more important, it is up to us to find the way to make love and kindness happen. We must purge the hatred form our hearts. We must turn to the Light and goodness within us. Meho's memory calls us to...

The Imam interrupts Nedjo , "Excuse me. This is a time for patience and perseverance. I beg you not to get involved. You will get these people overwrought."

Jusuf looks at Nedjo, who shrugs his shoulders, and then interrupts the Imam. "What do you mean? Should we be neutral?"

The Imam says, "It is the only way!"

Jusuf mumbles under his breath, "Never!"

The funeral party begins to move in a solemn procession toward a building in the cemetery.

The women gather for the "Te Whid." Aisha and a group of women, lead by the Bula, are holding their service.

The Bula reads, "Here is what the Garden, which the heedful are promised, will be like; rivers will flow through it; its food and its shade shall be perpetual. Such is the compensation for those who do their duty; while the outcome for disbelievers will be the Fire."

The Bula concludes their service, as the men return to the reception hall. A group of women continues to lament in the background. Jusuf hugs his mother and joins her in a receiving line. Nedjo stands in line to offer his condolences.

While Aisha is receiving the mourners, she whispers to Jusuf, "Where is your father? This is a grand occasion."

Jusuf is taken aback, "He's in his grave, Mama."

Aisha responds in confusion, "Why didn't he come back with you?"

Nedjo picks up on the conversation and crosses to the other side of Aisha, saying, "Meho has died, Aisha. He'll always be with you."

Aisha thanks him, "That's very comforting, but why is he so late?"

CHAPTER 14
Treasure

All that is left of Jusuf and Aisha's burned-out house and shop is a pile of ruble. They have not felt up to cleaning it up or searching for anything. The memories were too fresh and painful. However, they were lucky the fire did not touch the small laundry room under the house. That is where they live, and it serves all their needs.

Today, Jusuf and Aisha decide to rummage through the ruble. While searching Jusuf comes upon what looks like a corner of gold metal. He starts to move the heavy timbers and ruble that bury it. It is as if he is digging for pure gold. Finally, he reaches it. He brushes the snow and cinders away.

He lets out an elated, "Yes!"

Far beyond his personal strength, he reaches down and plucks the payload from its grave. It is only an old wood stove from the laundry-drying room in the attic. It is still intact.

Jusuf calls, "Mama, come look!"

Aisha moves quickly through the debris. When she sees it, she starts to cry.

After a few moments, Aisha says, "Allah be praised. That is just grand."

They start to drag the stove to the cellar laundry room.

Jusuf exclaims, "Tonight we shall have a warm place to sleep."

Aisha is filled with joy, "And I'll cook us a warm dinner of nettle soup."

This is their quality of life. An old wood stove is more precious than gold, and a bowl of warm nettle soup is a pure luxury.

As they drag the stove, some ruble moves, and Aisha sees something glitter. They stop, and she reaches down and moves some chard sticks. She tugs on a bit of fabric, which falls apart in her hand. Finally, she is able to slide it out very carefully. It is a charred and half-burned box, with a silver garland band around it.

Jusuf recognizes it and smiles. "It is for you. It's the present I had for you on Christmas."

She opens it excitedly. While much of the wrapping seems to disintegrate in her hands, she manages to remove the silver garland as it breaks apart in pieces. She sets each bit aside as though it is a precious treasure. As she gets closer to the prize, the paper is less and less burned. She unfolds the box and carefully lays it back. When she sees the brush, she picks it up with two fingers and holds it softly next to her chest. It is in perfect condition.

A deeply personal feeling shows on her face, as she reaches up and lets her hair free. Like a young woman in the intimacy of her own room, she brushes out her hair. Her face is radiant with inner pleasure. Then she turns slightly toward Jusuf, and lifting her head slightly to one side and looking at him out of the corner of her eye... She says coyly, "Do you like the way I look, my darling? Come here, Meho, I have a kiss for you."

Jusuf is shocked and embarrassed. He blurts out, "I'm not Meho! I'm Jusuf!"

She slips the brush into her apron pocket and quickly twists her hair up again.

Aisha says assuredly, "Of course you are. Of course you are. Come, my husband, let's take this grand stove to our shelter."

Jusuf rolls his eyes in disbelief.

They drag the stove to their shelter. Jusuf throws open the bulkhead and they carefully slide it down the steps and through the door.

Aisha touches it tenderly and says, "I'll have to give it a cleaning."

Jusuf responds, "OK. I'll go and see if I can find some bits of stovepipe. I think I can break a hole in the base of the chimney to hook it up. The chimney is still tall enough to draw the smoke. The vent in the wall is perfect to draw in air."

Aisha calls after him, "And don't forget, my dear, to bring us a good supply of that charcoal up there." She laughs.

Jusuf stops on the stairs and turns back to look at his mama. He smiles and thinks to himself, "That is the first time she has laughed since it happened. That's a good sign. Yes Nedjo, I'm thinking positive."

CHAPTER 15
Power Corrupts

It is a quiet night in early spring. The Serbian militia move silently into position around the Igman Arms Factory. Ranko is leading the assault, with Vladimir at his side. With a pair of binoculars, Ranko scans the perimeter. He pauses on the guardhouse and zooms in. A plant security guard is sound asleep in his chair. Ranko says to himself, "Just as I thought, thank you very much. Sleep on old man; you'll soon wake up in hell."

Via walkie-talkie, Ranko whispers, "This is command 1. All positions penetrate the perimeter and advance on designated targets."

He then signals Vladimir, who throws a hand grenade into the guardhouse. The security guard is startled awake, but he has no idea what just happened. All is silent and he starts to dose off again. The second his eyelids close…

The explosion of the grenade breaks the silence. The guardhouse blows apart, with pieces and body parts flying in every direction.

All hell breaks loose! The militia attacks the factory from every direction. Explosions rip the security fence apart. The alarm sounds, and security police appear in opposition. They take cover and return the automatic gunfire of the advancing militia. Bullets are flying everywhere, ricocheting off hard surfaces, ripping open cloth bags, splintering wooden boxes and pinning down the security police. At every pause, the security police pop out and return fire.

This triggers another barrage of automatic gunfire, with the same results. It takes the Serbian militia six repetitions of this scenario to figure out that they need to change positions to get a better angle on the security police. On the next barrage, they use the cover to move men in position. After that, one by one the security police are overpowered and taken out.

The militia moves swiftly through the plant, loading all weapons and ammunition on forklifts, hand trucks and dollies and quickly moving them to the loading area.

At points they are attacked by a hiding security policeman, and a shootout occurs. Within seconds, the militia surrounds the security policeman and his opposition is quickly removed.

Other militia, including Vladimir, move through the plant systematically planting plastic explosives in strategic locations.

Suddenly Vladimir comes under fire from the catwalk and he ducks for cover. He quickly locates the security policeman and they shoot it out. The security policeman is hit in the leg and moves out into the open. Vladimir sprays him with bullets. He flies backward and falls from the catwalk.

 Without warning, Vladimir goes into a Fairytale trance. The lights flash in his mind. The Fairytale appears and starts to play out in his mind. The Fairytale men at arms move about as if they were his

militia. But only Vladimir sees himself as the Young Prince and interacts with the men at arms.

In the Fairytale, the Prince taxes the people and hires men at arms. The soldiers not only collect the taxes, they take what they want. But in a back street of the village, the Prince is taking a shortcut to get to another section of the village, when a disgruntled trapper spots him and shoots him with his crossbow. He is mortally wounded, and the Young Prince finds him. When he is dying he speaks these last words to his son, "Please understand, my son, I must take my last six 'fuzzies' with me to the grave. They will help me in the hereafter. Now you shall be the Prince."

The Prince dies as the Young Prince (Vladimir) kneels over him.

The Young Prince shouts in anguish, "Father!"

The lights flash again in Vladimir's mind and the Fairytale and men at arms fade away...

As Vladimir comes out of the Fairytale, he scrambles for cover. He hides behind a stack of empty crates, shaking in fear.

The other members of Vladimir's team come to his aid, but they can't figure out what is wrong with him. Finally, they get his attention and convince him the coast is clear. They finish planting their explosives.

At the loading dock, the militia quickly loads the arms into trucks. The militia is like ants swarming all over the place. A stream of trucks has already started to move out the doors.

Ranko and Vladimir arrive at the loading dock at the same time. When Vladimir sees his father, he runs to him and throws his arms around him affectionately. He says, "I thought that you had been killed."

Ranko pushes him away coldly, "Of course I'm not. I can take care of myself. Mind what you're doing, such a display is unmanly and a sign of weakness."

Ranko turns and shouts an order to the last trucks, "Let's get them out of here!"

Vladimir stands for a moment crushed by his father's lack of love for him. Then he runs for a moving truck and jumps on.

As the last truck pulls out, Ranko jumps in his jeep and shouts to the driver, "Move it."

The militia, with Vladimir and Ranko, pass through the gate and up the road about a hundred meters.

Ranko commands his driver, "Stop here."

He stands and turns back toward the factory, with a trigger device in his hands.

Ranko says in a controlled vicious tone, "Now this is real power."

With an evil smile on his face, he presses the button. Where the factory once stood, a blinding white light flashes in the eyes of the militia.

The entire factory blows up and burns, with flames and debris flying high into the night sky.

As the flash fades, Ranko is silhouetted against the glow of the leaping flames.

CHAPTER 16
Destruction and Deception

High in the mountains overlooking Konjic, Vladimir is commanding a mortar position. It is a very dark summer night, and they are firing rounds into the village. Vladimir is directing their fire through a pair of binoculars.

Vladimir calls out, "Two degrees up; one degree left."

The target is the hospital. The mortar explodes on the side of the building.

Vladimir raises his hand in a fist and pulls his elbow down into his waist, saying, "Yes! Lock in those co-ordinances and let 'em fly. Give 'em hell!"

Doctors and nurses move frantically down the corridors of the hospital. They act quickly to move the patients to safety. Flying glass and plaster falls around them.

A nurse opens the door to a room to evacuate the patients. Just as she steps through the door, a mortar crashes through the window and explodes in the room. There is a flash of light and an explosion. Her body flies back through the door, across the corridor and into the opposite wall. Another nurse screams and rushes to her aid.

A doctor moves in and checks her quickly, "Leave her and get the living to safety first."

An orderly rushes into a room and loads all the monitoring apparatuses onto the patient's bed. He quickly unlocks the wheals and spins the bed around heading for the door. In the next instant, a mortar flies through the window and lands in front of him. He shouts as the explosion rips him, the patient and the room apart. A doctor flings open the door and there is nothing but a gaping hole in the side of the building. For a moment, he struggles to catch his balance and step back from the precipice.

The mortars stop. For thirty-five minutes, there is a deadly silence. In the next moment, the building and its occupants seem to take a deep breath. Then the silence is shattered by screams and the shouting of orders, along with the groans and creaking sounds of the building.

Back on the hill, Vladimir is preparing the men to move out. As he looks down the trail, he can see two figures approaching. He quickly raises his weapon and takes aim. Suddenly he realizes that it is General Jovanovic and Ranko and lowers his weapon. He calls his men to attention.

General Jovanovic and Ranko are casually making an inspection of the mortar positions.

Jovanovic calls Vladimir aside, "What's your target, son? And what's the status?"

Vladimir barks back, "The hospital, sir. We are able to take out most of the upper level from here."

Jovanovic laughs maniacally, "Excellent choice of target. The enemy shall have no comfort or aid anywhere or from anyone."

Vladimir snaps in agreement, "No, sir."

Jovanovic smiles, "Solder, I'm going to make you a corporal, keep up the good work. You have a real future in the Serbian army."

Vladimir snaps a salute, which the General returns before moving off to inspect the men. Ranko stays behind.

Ranko pats Vladimir on the back, "I'm proud of you, Corporal. You're a credit to the Rakic name and my command."

He then holds out his hand to shake hands with him. There is no love or warmth in his praise. The expression on Vladimir's face goes from joy to despair in a second. Then he snaps to attention and salutes his father. Ranko thinks nothing of it and is very comfortable in just returning the salute. As Ranko follows the General, the lights flash in Vladimir's mind and he goes into a Fairytale trance.

The Fairytale emerges in his mind. The people in the village are going about their daily business. Vladimir sees himself as the Young Prince.

He and his knights are engaging in an attack on a neighboring village. As they ride through the village, they slay everything in sight, men, women and children. The people scream and rush frantically for cover. The Young Prince shows no emotion. The blood from a victim splashes on his cheek and he doesn't bother to wipe it away.

In the Fairytale from that day on, the Young Prince becomes even worse than his father. He becomes a tyrant. He learns the ways of war and fights and kills for greater conquest. He and his knights become rich with plunder. There is no prize too small that it isn't worth the killing.

One day, the Young Prince captures a beautiful Princess as they take a castle. The castle guards try to defend her, but he chops them down, with his broad sword.

The Princess screams and struggles trying to get free, but he hits her and knocks her unconscious. He then drags her by the hair to his horse, like a primitive cave man.

He hardens his heart to love and even his bride is just another conquest. A darkness spreads over the

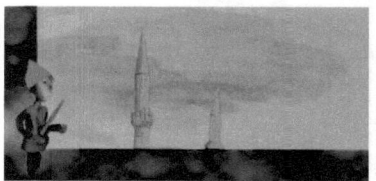

land. A bitter cold wind blows and freezes the heart of every living thing.

As the light flashes in Vladimir's mind, the knights and villagers start to disappear and the Fairytale begins to fade away.

The last image we can see is Vladimir's silhouette against the stormy night sky. And the ruins of the burning hospital buildings loom up behind him.

CHAPTER 17
Mind Tricks

The stove that Jusuf and Aisha found in the burned-out ruins of the house now sits proudly in the corner of their shelter. It gives them warmth and a place to cook and heat water. It is hard for them to imagine how they could survive without it. Yet one look at the shelter makes one wonder how they can manage with so little.

The basement shelter was once the laundry room where Aisha earned a small extra income. It is only a small space about 3.5 by 4 meters. This is where they sleep, cook and eat. The old laundry machine sits idle between their WW II army cots, because there is no longer any electric power. It now functions as a table for the oil lamp. There is one very small window high on the wall and a small door opening to the stairs and bulkhead to the outside.

The place is immaculate and free of clutter, but of course, they don't have many things to create clutter. On the wall are two hooks, containing one change of clothes for each of them. Aisha's hairbrush lies on the makeshift table next to the oil lamp. Aside from the two cots, the only other furniture in the room is a small stool.

Jusuf is sound asleep on one of the cots. Slowly he begins to wake up. He rubs his eyes and looks around for Aisha, who is gone.

He calls out, "Mama?"

There is no response. He looks over at her cot. She made it neatly.

Jusuf anxiously calls out louder and lauder, "Mama. Mama! MAMA!"

He quickly pulls out his rolled up clothes, which are under his cot, and dresses. He rushes out the door, up the steps, throws open the bulkhead and runs outside looking in every direction. He is frantic, but she is not to be found or seen.

Suddenly, the lights flash in his mind and the Fairytale images and people start to appear. Jusuf tries to resist, but the Fairytale and his real action start to overlap. This becomes more and more irritating for him.

In the Fairytale very few people give away 'fuzzies' any more. If anyone dares to try to give one away, others mock and belittle them.

Jusuf runs down the road. He sees a farmer, trying to rebuild his barn by himself.

He stops and calls up to the farmer, "Have you seen my mother go by?"

The farmer responds in a puzzled tone, without looking at Jusuf, "She went down the road early this morning. It was very strange. She was friendly and waved."

Six villagers come up the road and stand next to Jusuf. They too look up at the farmer repairing his barn.

The Carpenter (Jusuf) turns to the villagers and suggests, "Let us stay and help this neighbor rebuild his barn." Jusuf slaps himself, because he is in search of his mom.

 Then one of the villagers says, "And who is going to pay us for this? Totally impractical! Don't be absurd!

Another villager chimes in, "We are so few and the barn is so big!" The villagers all turn and continue up the road.

Jusuf looks at the farmer and shrugs his shoulders. The farmer offers him a hammer. Jusuf says apologetically, "I really must go and find my mother. She is not well in her head."

The farmer nods, with a sarcastic expression and goes back to his work.

Jusuf hurries down the road.

After a while, he sees a woman putting up a new sign over the entrance of a theatre tent.

Jusuf stops and asks the woman, "Did my mother go by your theatre?"

The woman responds with a smile, "I saw her pass some time ago. She stopped to say hello. Not many do that these days." Then she turns back to her task.

Jusuf turns to head down the road and three busybodies confront him.

The first one says, "You know you can't trust theatre people!"

The second one comments rhetorically, "Who's going to watch our homes while we are at work all day?

The third one asks, "Where are they going to stay? Not near me!"

The first one buzzes in a whisper, "Did you notice that some of them are left-handed?"

The second buzzes back, "A definite sign of low moral character."

Jusuf shakes his head and shouts at them, "Give me a break!" He tries to shake it off. He then pushes his way through them and continues down the road.

In the center of town now, Jusuf comes up the street and stops in front of the rectory. The priest is standing at the window looking down. He is always

 there keeping track of everything that is going on.

Jusuf calls up to him, "Father, did you see my mom pass by?"

The priest shouts down angrily, "I don't have time to stand here and look after every person who walks by."

Jusuf shakes his head, smiles and waves.

As Jusuf starts to walk away, the priest throws open the window and calls after him, "I'm sorry; she doesn't belong to our church."

Jusuf does a double take. Now he sees himself as the Dark-haired Child. He smiles and calls back, "Thanks anyway, Father." He turns away and gives himself a whack on the back of his head to try to get out of the Fairytale.

Down the road, Jusuf passes the school. It is under attack. He dodges the bullets and runs down the street. He jumps between two houses. The bullets bounce off the walls and shower him with wood and plaster. He crouches in a corner and covers his face.

The Fairytale people torment him and their cynicism seems to cut him apart.

The cynic stands aloof over him, "Well, that is one less 'fuzzy' in the world. How dumb can you get!"

The rationalizer cops a pious attitude, "How do you expect to get into heaven without at least one 'fuzzy'?"

Jusuf screams louder and louder, "No. NO! No more!"

Jusuf fights off the Fairytale, trying to calm himself down. He takes several deep breaths, blowing out air and letting his lungs fill again. Each breath becomes slower and longer.

The gunfire stops, but Jusuf can hear voices. He sticks out his head to peek around the corner. He sees a Serbian militiaman coming his way. He ducks back. He then hears a barrage of gun shots.

The Serb falls motionless to the pavement.

The gunshots stop. Jusuf looks out again. He sees that the Serb is shot. Without hesitation, Jusuf runs out to him. It is a boy his own age, who he knows. He is badly wounded.

The Serb Boy reaches up and takes Jusuf's shirt, "Help me!"

Jusuf picks him up and carries him quickly down the street, but the Fairytale people haunt him.

The cynic says, "He's going to help a war victim."

Jusuf snaps back at the cynic, "Maybe you should help!"

The rationalizer chants back, "Why should we help? It is not our problem. We didn't make it happen."

Jusuf shouts at the Fairytale people, "Enough! Get lost!" The light flashes in Jusuf's head and the Fairytale image and people disappear.

Jusuf hurries down the street toward the hospital, carrying the boy. His determination is so strong the weight of the Serb Boy seems to have no effect on him. Twenty minutes later, he steps over and around debris in the street and enters the emergency room at the hospital.

The conditions in the hospital are appalling. Exhausted nurses and doctors are racing about the corridors, which are lined with patients in beds. Jusuf tries to get help for the boy in his arms, but everyone is busy.

Some of the doctors and nurses walk past him. Jusuf tries to get their attention, but they hurry through a double door, which swings back in his face.

Aisha comes up behind him. She is wearing a nurse's uniform. Aisha asks, "Do you need help?"

Jusuf spins around explaining, "This boy has been shot! Can you..." When he comes face to face with his mother, he is speechless.

An orderly comes down the corridor with a gurney.

Jusuf stutters out, "...Mama?"

Aisha says calmly, "Put him down here on the gurney, Meho, we can take care of him."

Jusuf puts the boy on the gurney, and says, "It's me, Mama, Jusuf! I've been looking all over for you."

Aisha says with total clarity, "I know it's you."

Jusuf is relieved, "Please come home."

Aisha answers with compassion, "I'm needed here."

Jusuf is becoming curious, "I didn't know you were a nurse."

Aisha responds with maternal authority, "It's good I am, with all the senseless killing. Jusuf, you must promise that you will never kill anyone. Human life is far too precious. I'll be home tonight." She turns away to the boy on the gurney. "I must get him to the surgery at once." Looking back at Jusuf, she says, "You know, for a minute there, you looked like Meho, when we first met here at the hospital twenty-four years ago. It was love at first sight, and he was a grand sight. Believe me."

Jusuf is surprised at her cognitive response. He stands and looks after her as she wheels off the gurney.

CHAPTER 18
Deadly Choices

One of the most picturesque places in all of Mostar is the old bridge, which connects the two halves of the city. The construction took place during the Ottoman Empire from 1558-1566, with its majestic arch spanning the Neretva river. The two impressive towers that stand on either side traditionally house the "guardians" of the bridge.

This bridge has survived numerous regional conflicts, Turkish occupation, two World Wars and the Cold War, with Russian occupation. It is a symbol of its people's endurance in the face of conflict. It is a monument to the peaceful collaboration of three ethnic groups.

On this morning, the sky is blackened with storm clouds and pelting rain. A bolt of lightning flashes in the sky and strikes a tall tree fifty meters north of the bridge. It splinters into pieces and almost instantly explodes with a deafening thunderclap. Mother Nature is not pleased with what is about to happen.

Ranko, Vladimir and the Serbian militia are holding a position on one side of the bridge. The Muslim militia is holding a position on the other side of the bridge. The Croatian militia is holding the center of the bridge, barricaded in with sandbags and makeshift armament. If you were standing in one of the nearby mosque towers, you would find it impossible to tell who is who. The mystery is that the fighters can't tell either, so they are not sure who they are trying to kill at any given moment.

Ranko motions for Vladimir to come to him.

Vladimir runs in a crouched position to where Ranko is observing the field.

Ranko points to a guardian house on their side of the bridge. He instructs Vladimir, "Take your platoon and cleanse that guardian house. Then set up a mortar position to take out the bridge."

Vladimir snaps back without thinking, "Yes, sir."

Vladimir motions to his men and they move cautiously toward the guardian house, crouching and dodging obstacles, while trying not to be seen. They fire repeatedly into the windows, but there is no return fire. Shattering glass and debris fly in every direction. They quickly scramble toward the entrance door and take up positions outside of the house. Vladimir motions for some of his men to take up positions around the guardian house at every level.

A Croatian soldier, on the bridge, spots the movement of Vladimir and his men. He watches what's happening for a minute and then puts two and two together. He shouts, "That's my house!"

He starts to climb over the barrier to go home, but his buddy grabs his belt and holds him back.

The Croatian soldier struggles in protest, "My wife and kids are in there!"

His buddy pulls him back, saying, "It would be suicide!"

When his men are in position, Vladimir kicks in the door, and four members of his team move inside with him. There is no one to be seen. Vladimir looks in a small empty room where there is only a cloth covering a pile of ruble. He then moves on. The team moves cautiously from room to room, seeing nothing.

The Croatian struggles to get free from his buddy. He screams at Vladimir, "My babies! You Serbian pigs!"

His buddy holds on to him tightly, "There's noth'n you can do."

Vladimir hears a sound coming from the empty room. He moves back cautiously and stops outside the door. All is silent. He turns to move away, but then he hears a muffled cry. He turns back quickly and throws open the door. The room is just as before. All he can hear is the storm raging on the outside and the rain pouring in the shattered window. Vladimir stands studying the cloth-covered pile of ruble.

The Croatian breaks loose from his buddy in a crazy frenzy, shouting at the Serbians, "You bastards! I'll kill you all!" He falls over the top of the barricade, gets up and runs onto the Serbian line, firing everywhere.

He is oblivious to his Buddy shouting after him, "You stupid son-of-a-bitch, get down."

Some of the Croatian's wild gunfire ricochets off his guardian house.

Three of the ricocheting bullets fly through the open window, hit the ceiling and fall to the floor. Vladimir flinches, but notices that the cloth on the ruble moving slightly.

The Croatian is cut down from every
direction. His body flies jerkily in one direction then
another before falling motionless to the bridge road.

Vladimir quickly pulls off the cloth. There
huddled underneath is a Croatian woman, with two
small children and a baby in her arms. The children
are tucked in around her, like chicks under a hen.
Slowly Vladimir backs up to the doorway. He
hesitates, then pulls a hand grenade from his belt and
pulls the pin. He drops it inside the room, closes the
door and ducks for cover. His face goes from military
emotionless to regret and horror in a nanosecond. He
races back to the door screaming, "Nooooooo!"

The mother screams in terror and then the
children all start crying at once, with the whaling of
the baby rising above it all. The mother struggles to
her feet and tries to through herself on the hand
grenade.

The children call out for her, "Mama! Mama!
Mama!"

The Mother spreads out her arms. She is
almost th…

Just as Vladimir reaches the door, the grenade
explodes blowing the door off its hinges and driving
Vladimir to the floor.

Two of his team come to his rescue and pull
the door off him.

They help Vladimir to his feet, and he appears
to be uninjured.

Vladimir turns and looks in the room. The
gory mess of his handy work is more than he can

handle. He screams in agony and vomits all over the floor.

His team is more repulsed with the vomit than the heinous butchery of innocent women and children.

There is a barrage of lightning flashes all around the bridge and a defining roar of thunder.

The fighting begins. Bullets fly in every direction. There is killing and more killing and needles killing!

All sides launch their mortars.

Explosions rip apart the bridge and many of the lives that are on it.

The blood runs like rain down the gutters and into the river.

The Neretva runs red with the blood of its people. And its waters swallow up the pieces of the fallen bridge.

In less time than it takes to read this, the old Mostar Bridge is no more!

CHAPTER 19
Old Friends

High above the fields overlooking Konjic,
Vladimir's platoon is hiding in the tree line. It is a
beautiful autumn day, with full sunshine and a cool
breeze. Jusuf and Aisha are walking in the fields.

For the Muslims it is Ramazanski Bajram.
The fast of Ramadan is over. Jusuf is picking plums,
and Aisha is picking fall flowers.

Jusuf is whistling a tune. His old cloth
shopping bag is almost full. He pauses for a moment
to eat one of the plums, closing his eyes and turning
his face to the sun.

Aisha is humming the same tune. She notices
a bee in one of the flowers she is about to pick. She
reaches down to shoo it away with a very slow motion
of the back of her hand, saying, "Excuse me brother
bee. You have had enough from that little darling."
The bee calmly flies on to another flower.

There is the distant sound of shells exploding
in the village, and every now and then the chatter of
automatic weapons. No, that is not a celebration.
The war goes on and on.

Aisha looks up at the sun and stretches out her
arms. She says loudly, "I am so happy for such a
grand, quiet and peaceful day."

Jusuf responds in a loud whisper, "Mama,
keep your voice down."

She pays no attention to him and starts to sing
the Muslim song "Pismo," which makes Jusuf very
nervous. He is jumping at every sound. When he

scares up a pheasant, Aisha doesn't even react, but he flies through the air and knocks her to the ground.

Aisha calmly asks, "Why are you so jumpy? It was just a pheasant."

She stands and casually straightens herself. Jusuf rises cautiously, looking around. He pauses for a moment and studies the tree line in the hill above them, and then looks on.

Vladimir and his platoon lie very still and well hidden. Vladimir is watching them through binoculars.

One of his militiamen takes aim; Vladimir gently lays his hand on top of the rifle blocking his sights. Vladimir whispering, "Hold your fire. You'll give away our position."

The militiaman whispers in response, "Sure, he was your best friend. Our orders were to cleanse the area; we should kill them both."

Vladimir shifts his rifle pointing it in his face and says, "I told you to hold your fire! Any more questions?"

The militiaman slowly shakes his head, no.

Aisha looks down the hill to a farmhouse about two hundred meters away. She sees something. She says joyfully, "Look Rabia and Assim are sunning themselves with their two children. Isn't that grand!"

She waves and calls to them, but there is no response. "Hi, Rabia. Hi, Assim. Yoo-hoo!"

Jusuf tries to move her along down the path. Trying to distract her, he says, "Come on Mama! They can't hear you."

Aisha resists, so he takes her by the arm and pulls her along.

She loudly protests every step of the way, "Stop tugging on me. You don't need to be so rude. What is your rush anyway?"

Jusuf continues to try to move her along and get her out of the sight of the farmhouse.

Down the hill, at the peaceful little farmhouse, Aisha has seen the dead decaying bodies of Rabia, Assim and their two children. The crows fly in and out feeding on their bodies.

CHAPTER 20
Nothing is Sacred

Partially concealed, Vladimir is behind a small tool shed in a park overlooking the Library of Konjic. He has a clear sightline on the library, which he is studying through his binoculars.

It is now winter and the first signs of snow have appeared in the mountains. The moonlight is the only illumination and it shimmers eerily in the blackened village.

Vladimir starts to go into the Fairytale. He sees the usual flashing of lights in his mind's eye. The Fairytale images begin to appear along with a group of medieval soldiers engaged in battle. The action draws Vladimir in as the Young Prince.

The Young Prince, in the midst of a raging battle, is cutting down knights right and left. He is very skilled with a sword and shows no mercy. As he  takes on the last of the King's guard the fight becomes more intense. The guard parries every blow he strikes. And the Young Prince parries every strike upon himself. Blow on blow, strike on strike, it goes back and forth. The tempo builds and grows more intense. Vladimir feels the perspiration pouring down his face inside the helmet. The Prince tries every trick in the book, but gains no advantage. Then by some fluke of fate, a bit of ice falls from the tree onto the helmet of the King's guard.

In that split second of distraction, the Prince thrusts his sword through the armor and into the Knight's heart.

Finally, he is face to face with the old King of this land. The King quickly considers himself no match for this Young Prince and kneels before him. Pleading, he says, "I beg your mercy, my Liege."

The Young Prince shouts, "Pay me homage, or die."

The old King responds, still with a pleading tone, "I can only pay homage to God, but you can have all that is mine to give, including my kingdom."

But those that would not give the Prince homage and worshiping him, he destroyed in the cruelest way imaginable.

The Young Prince puts out the King's eyes and cuts off his hands and feet.

Vladimir tries to fight off the Fairytale, screaming, "NO! This is not me!" Finally, as he comes out of the Fairytale, he tries to shake off what he has done. Slowly the Fairytale images fade away.

His actions in the Fairytale repulse him. He cannot accept what he has done and tries to free himself from the memory of it. Then he hears the sound of his father's voice on his walkie-talkie.

"Nightjar, come in. Come in, Nightjar. This is Eagle 2 calling Nightjar."

Vladimir fumbles with his walkie-talkie and then responds, "Nightjar, here. I read you, Eagle 2."

Ranko, who has been calling for over a minute, says with an at last tone in his voice, "Are you in position?"

Vladimir responds, "A ringside seat."

Ranko is standing near a 120-millimeter artillery cannon. His team is shoving home a large shell and closing the breach.

Ranko says in the walkie-talkie, "I'll fire a round. You give the correction."

Vladimir responds, "Affirmative."

Ranko signals for the cannon to fire the first round. The roar of the cannon is deafening and it jumps back in recoil. One of the team members just barely gets out of the way.

Vladimir can hear the whistling of the shell coming in overhead. It explodes, taking out the corner of a nearby house. There is screaming and scrambling of innocent people inside the house.

Vladimir does a quick calculation on a piece of paper and gives the corrected coordinates into the walkie-talkie, "Three degrees down, eight degrees right.

Ranko's team loads another shell and slams the breach home. He reads them the corrections, and the men quickly adjust the cannon.

The next shell comes whistling overhead and takes out a store on the other side of the library. People in the street are screaming and running for shelter. A siren starts howling to warn everyone in town, as if the explosions haven't already done that.

Vladimir figures out the next coordinates and calls it in, "Four degrees left."

A shell whistles in and hits the side of the library closest to Vladimir. He makes the final correction.

The cannon team loads the next shell smoother than the others. They are quickly getting the hang of it and working more like a team.

Vladimir calls in the correction, "One degree up and one degree right. That should be bingo. Everything else can be a half a degree plus or minus."

The shells whistle in one right after the other and pound the library to ruble.

Vladimir starts to retreat from his position and comes under fire. He ducks behind a statue of Tito. A sniper has set up a machine gun in the house where the first shell hit and she has spotted Vladimir. Every time Vladimir tries to move, she opens fire. He tries to return the fire, but she is too well concealed behind the blown out walls of the house. Vladimir huddles behind the statue and frantically works out a calculation on his paper. When the shelling on the library stops...

Vladimir calls into the walkie-talkie, "Eagle 2, this is Nightjar. I've been pinned down by a sniper. Adjust coordinates to two degrees up and four degrees left."

Ranko shouts back, "Stay put, the garbage will soon be history."

Another shell cuts through the silence and the house where the sniper is hiding raises off its foundation and collapses in a pile of ruble.

Vladimir calls back, "Mission accomplished!" He then runs for the hills.

CHAPTER 21
Making News

Why is it that warring societies have complete disregard for their enemy's accumulated knowledge? Could it be that any assumed value in war is nothing but a myth and the reality behind all war is nothing but hatred pour and simple?

The next morning the sun rises on a pile of ruble where the library once stood. The UN Peacekeepers and Serbian troops led by Jovanovic march up the street and take positions around the smoldering demolished library. They are here to defend the... They are here to... Exactly why are they here? The library is nothing but a pile of ruble. There is not one whole stone, brick or piece of paper in the whole mountain of debris. Then out of the clear blue, everything becomes clear.

The American NBC press corps news van pulls up and parks in front of the library ruble.

The camera crew gets out and starts to set up the cameras. They run the cables, set up microphones and lights with reflectors or diffusers.

Ana and Ranko are sitting in the news van. A star reporter is coaching them for a TV interview with NBC News. We can see that Ana has dressed for the occasion, bundled in her finest fur coat, and Ranko is now dressed in civilian clothes.

The correspondent reads from her notes, "I will ask about your mixed marriage, and your feelings about the ethnic cleansing. Then I'll ask about your reaction to the shelling of the library. And be sure you use your words like "horror of this act" and "heinous atrocity." Also, remember to be as emotional as possible. The people will like that."

Ana looks at Ranko for approval; Ranko looks at Ana with a smirk. Turning to the correspondent, they nod in agreement. The correspondent mistakenly reads the smirk as a sexual flirtation.

The cameraman sticks his head in the door. The correspondent asks him, "Are you ready?"

The cameraman grins, "I'm always ready." Then he laughs at his own joke.

Everyone piles out of the van. The makeup and wardrobe people go to work getting them primped for the shoot.

The cameraman studies the scene one last time and changes his mind. He motions to the crew to refocus the camera five meters to the left and move the mic and light diffusers.

He turns to the correspondent pointing out the location, "Can you move them over there? The light will be absolutely perfect in that spot."

The correspondent herds everybody to the indicated position. Makeup and wardrobe continue working, focusing mainly on the correspondent now.

The cameraman arranges everybody in their spots and marks it with a bit of chalk. He then takes light readings with the light-meter hanging around his neck. As he walks back to the camera, he trips over the broken head of a statue, which is in the library ruble. He motions for one of the crew to come and turns to study his picture. He turns to the crewmember and points out exactly where he wants her to move the head in the background of his shot. Finally, he goes back to his camera and adjusts the light settings. He turns to the crew and gives them a thumbs up. They return the signal. Makeup and wardrobe clear the picture.

The cameraman calls to the correspondent, "O.K. Let's get this down."

Everyone adjusts their look for the camera. The correspondent relaxes and puts on a natural friendly concerned look. Ana and Ranko pose stiffly and artificially for the camera.

The cameraman smiles at them and calls out, "Rolling!"

The correspondent looks into the camera, "During the night another senseless atrocity has occurred in the small town of Konjic. Behind me lie the ruins of the public library. Not one page of knowledge or one precious relic remains. Here to talk to us about this disaster are two of the leading members of this community, Ana and Ranko Rakic. In an ethnic war that defies logic, theirs is a marriage worth noting. Ana, tell us about your marriage?

Ana is stiff and unnatural in front of the camera, "Ranko and I have been married for over twenty years. He is a Serb and I'm a Croat. I get a lot of pleasure from him. I never think of him as a Serb. I only think of him as Ranko."

Ranko is anxious to get in the limelight, "As for myself, we've always been good together."

Ana strikes a glamorous pose, "I don't understand all this ethnic-cleansing business."

Ranko puffs himself up, "I think of myself as a Yugoslav not a Serb. I wish that all the ethnic groups could respect us."

The correspondent turns to them, "How do you feel about what happened to the library?"

Ana is a little more natural in her response, "It's a horror. It's unthinkable that such a thing could happen. After all this is part of our culture. Many of the old books and documents are irreplaceable. In fact…"

Ranko cuts in, 'This is a heinous atrocity. I, myself, had donated many volumes to the library. What possible military value could the destruction of a library have? I recently put on display the pictures and mementos from my mother-in-law's skating career."

The correspondent turns to Ana, "Ana, can you tell us about your mother?" Before Ana can answer, she interrupts. "Just a minute, you have something on your cheek."

She pretends to wipe it away with her mitten. While doing this she deliberately pushes the fuzzy mitten into her eye. Ana flinches and covers her eyes. When she takes her hands away, there are tears in her eyes.

The cameraman says to himself, "Sneaky lady. Where'd you learn that little trick?"

The correspondent is proud of herself. "We're rolling, Ana! Can you tell us about your mother?"

Ana is crying, and Ranko gives her his handkerchief.

Ana becomes naturally choked up, "My mother was an Olympic medalist in figure skating and she and my father were killed in Belgrade a year ago. All her photographs, medals, skates and things were destroyed in the shelling."

The correspondent turns to the camera, "There you have it. Now we know how Cleopatra felt when they burned her library. This is another senseless act of violence, destroying everything that has any value or meaning to the people of Konjic." She turns to Ana and Ranko, "I want to thank you for taking the time to share your reactions to this atrocity." She pauses and turns to the cameraman, "O.K. That's a cut." She shakes Ana's hand and then Ranko's. "Thank you for coming out this morning. You have been most helpful."

Ana and Ranko start to walk down the street toward their limo.

The cameraman gives his team the O.K. sign and then gestures to them instructions.

The press corps starts to reposition the camera and lighting.

The correspondent says to the cameraman, "When we get to the trailer, cut the bit with the mitten in the eye. We can set up back here to tape some closing remarks and get some detail shots, which you can cut in at the end. Then we can send it."

CHAPTER 22
Christmas Morning

It is Christmas again in Aisha and Jusuf's shelter. A pine bough hangs on the wall, covered tastefully with bits of colored paper cut in different shapes. Next to it hangs an old picture of the Virgin Mary. The Islam faith holds Mary in very high regard and even mentions her in The Quran. She is very special to Aisha, so this picture now hangs here year round.

It is a year since Meho was shot and their home and shop burned. The room is lit with a stubby candle. There is no longer any oil for their lamp or water, and the electric fixtures hang idle as a reminder of what once was.

Aisha is sitting on her old army cot wrapping a small package in a piece of old paper. She ties it with the bit of charred garland that once adorned the hairbrush that Jusuf gave her. As she finishes, she hears someone coming.

For a moment she is startled and her face shows the fear of potential disaster. Jusuf opens the door and quickly comes into the shelter and closes the door. Aisha freezes still.

Jusuf sees his mama's fear, "It's just me."

Aisha's face relaxes and she smiles. Jusuf shakes the snow from his clothes. He is carrying a small bundle of wood. Before he can take off his coat, Aisha wishes him a "Merry Christmas."

She stands and presents him with the small package.

Jusuf is very surprised, "Where did you get a present for me?"

Aisha giggles gleefully, "You'll have to open it and see."

He carefully unties the ribbon and removes the paper without tearing it. Jusuf is amazed, because they have no money. He pulls back the paper and exclaims, "It's a pair of wool socks!"

Aisha explains apologetically, "They're an old pair of Meho's which I found, but I mended them and washed the smell of the fire out of them. I hope you like them."

Jusuf holding them to his heart, "I love them! They're wonderful." He gives his mother a big kiss. Then he says, "I've a small gift for you, but it isn't so fancy wrapped."

He reaches inside his coat and takes something out, which is wrapped in old newspaper, and presents the package to Aisha.

She slowly opens the newspaper, and inside she finds his handkerchief wrapped around the contents. Before unfolding it, she says, "I hope your handkerchief was clean." She then unfolds it with her eyes closed. When she opens them and looks, her jaw drops open. She looks like she has just received the most valuable gift of her life. Tears role down her cheeks as she exclaims, "Allah be praised, its grass and three roots! How grand!"

Jusuf is pleased, "I'm glad you like them."

Aisha places her hand on his heart, "I'm very happy for these. I'll cook them right now for breakfast." Aisha is troubled and down. She finally confesses, "I miss Meho so much." She holds back her tears and then turns to the stove.

They are starving and a handful of grass with a few roots becomes a banquet.

Jusuf doesn't know what to say and turns away. He walks over and sits on his cot. His face is distraught, and his eyes distant. He musters courage.

What Jusuf doesn't know is that Vladimir is about to have the same vision that he is about to have. Vladimir is lying in bed staring at the ceiling.

Jusuf's mind spins off into the world of the Riddle of Leadership, which Nedjo has told him and Vladimir. He begins to see someone walking barefoot in the snow, up in the hills. The person is bundled up in tattered clothes and bent over. He looks down and it is as if he is following him in his footprints. Then they hear the sound of a lamb crying. They look up and listen. It is then that Jusuf sees that the person in front of him is Vladimir. They hurry to the edge of the cliff and look down. Below they see the wolf dragging the lamb in the snow. Vladimir turns and they lock eyes. There is a question on his face, what shall we do? Jusuf doesn't know what to say, and shrugs his shoulders.

The vision slowly fades from Jusuf's mind, and he sits there staring at the wall. Jusuf mumbles to himself, "What are we supposed to do?" Jusuf shrugs his shoulders and wonders if Vladimir knows what to do. The tears well up in his eyes.

He turns to Aisha and tries to convince his mother, "We'll be all right, Mama, and things'll get better."

They sit in silence, eating the grass and roots, which Aisha has prepared.

Aisha slowly comes back to herself again, and asks, "Do you think it's safe for me to go for water? We're almost out."

Jusuf cheerfully responds, "I'll go. I know a safe place, further down the river, and I can carry more."

Aisha is anxious to get out, "Well, I'll at least come up and see the sun. That would be grand."

They put on their coats and climb up out of the shelter closing the door behind them. Jusuf takes with him two empty jugs and hikes off to his new water spot. Aisha looks around and then stands very still.

Aisha says, "What a grand dove. I haven't seen one of them in months."

Very slowly she raises her hand, and the bird flies down and perches on her outstretched arm.

Aisha talks to the dove very tenderly, "I know you're looking for food but there is none, not for you anyway."

With a quick move, she seizes the bird. Still talking tenderly to it, "You will make a grand dinner."

Nedjo watches Aisha as he approaches the shelter and comes up behind her. He is wearing his vision device and carrying a basket.

His footsteps startle Aisha. As she turns around, she is relieved to see that it is Nedjo. She quickly puts the dove under her coat.

Nedjo hold out the basket, "I brought you a few apples and vegetables." He hands her the basket loaded to overflowing. Aisha is very excited.

Aisha begins to go through the basket, "It will make a grand feast. I haven't seen an onion in four months."

Jusuf returns with two jugs full of water. He is very happy to see Nedjo and drops the jugs to give him a big hug.

Aisha shows him the basket and holds up the onion, "Look, an onion! Tonight we shall have a feast. Nedjo, will you honor us by staying?"

She takes the dove from under her coat, and Jusuf sees it. He asks, "What are you going to do with that?"

Aisha says sheepishly, "It flew down into my hand, and I'm going to cook it for dinner, of course."

Jusuf reacts, "As wonderful as it would be to have meat, I couldn't eat it. On this holy day, it is a sign of the peace and love of Muhammad. It came to you, because it knew that it was safe with you. It is better to set it free or peace may never return to this land. Isn't that right Nedjo?

Aisha looks at Nedjo for approval.

Nedjo responds, "Your son is very wise."

Aisha looks at the dove. Then she takes a bite from an apple and removes it from her mouth.

Aisha says to the dove, "Yes, you knew there would be food for you. Here is a bit of apple." She gives it to the dove and opens her hand so that it can fly away. Their eyes follow the dove as it flies high up into the hills. Aisha smiles, "She probably has a man to feed." Turning to Jusuf and Nedjo, she says, "Let's go in and get warm."

They open the bulkhead and walk down the steps, through the door and into the shelter, closing everything tightly behind them.

Nedjo takes the Fairytale device from his backpack, "I have been working on the Fairytale device, and would like to try and bring Jusuf out of the Fairytale.

Jusuf needs no encouragement. He quickly puts it on. Aisha starts to prepare the food.

Jusuf says to Nedjo, "Great! I can't wait. It never happens at a good time!" Then adding quickly, "Not that I don't like your Fairytale."

Nedjo explains, "I have programmed the device to perform a formatting function. I hope it will erase what it has loaded into your subconscious." He plugs the device into a battery pack and then presses the buttons on the control box.

Jusuf reacts, "How did you know we didn't have power?"

"No one has power on this side of the village. I want you to describe what you feel." Nedjo adjusts Jusuf's headset so two diodes rest on his temples.

"OK, there is a tingling sensation at my temples. It's very similar to what I felt the first time. Now, I see red and yellow streaks on a blue-black background. The streaks are twisting and turning into different shapes. There is no other picture. Oops!

Everything went blank and there is no feeling at the temples any longer."

Nedjo smiles confidently, and helps him off with the headset. He says, "That should do it."

Unfortunately, it is wishful thinking, because Jusuf starts to go into a Fairytale trance after a few seconds. The lights flash before his eyes and the Fairytale scene fades in along with the Fairytale people.

Over the years, the small village sinks deeper and deeper into a gloomy darkness, until the magic of the 'warm fuzzies' is all but forgotten.

Nedjo can see that he has gone into the Fairytale. His face is filled with concern. He takes Jusuf's hand. Jusuf comes out of the Fairytale. The Fairytale images and Fairytale people fade out.

Nedjo tries to comfort Jusuf, "There is nothing in the Fairytale that can hurt you, so you shouldn't be frightened. Of course, it would be more comfortable not to have these trances all the time."

"That's for sure, but I really want to know how it ends. Does it have a happy ending?"

"Yes, it does, but I'm optimistic that I'll soon come up with something to get you both out of it."

Jusuf reacts on the words, "get you both out." His lips form the words over and over, until... He mumbles, "Have you seen... Have you... Is?"

Nedjo says, "Then I can tell you both how it ends."

Jusuf says, "I would like that."

Although there is confidence in Nedjo's voice, it only partially conceals his concern.

CHAPTER 23
Killing and Birth

In town, the Catholic Church is holding the Christmas services. Their Christmas carols fill the air for blocks around and the choir sings selected pieces from Handel's "Messiah." The whole scene creates an uplifting feeling of hope.

However, on the roof of a nearby building, a Muslim sniper takes a position, sets up his sniper rifle and begins to adjust the scope.

In this war, nothing is holy. Vladimir conceals himself near the Catholic Church. He lifts his rifle and takes aim on the Muslim sniper, who is poised and waiting. Before he can shoot, Vladimir goes into a Fairytale trance. He tries to fight it off, but to no avail.

The lights flash in his mind's eye and the Fairytale scene and Fairytale people start to appear.

The Young Prince is in a tall tower looking down from the parapet. He is shooting everyone in sight, with a crossbow. The ground below is piled with bodies one on the other. It looks like the last judgment. Vladimir fights to free himself of the image.

The lights flash in his mind and continue to flicker through the following. The Fairytale people fade in and out repeatedly.

The sound of the organ postlude begins.

An old Croatian man comes out of the church. He is buttoning his coat as the sniper takes aim.

The old man starts down the steps. A shot rings out and the old man grabs his chest and falls to the steps and rolls down. Two old Croatian women, hearing the shot, come rushing out of the church. They look in both directions and see no one. Then they hurry down the steps to help the old man. Two more shots ring out and the old women fall to the ground on top of the old man.

Vladimir tries to take aim on the Muslim sniper again. He has him in his sights, but then in the midst of the flashes and flickers, he sees Jusuf's face as the Old Carpenter in the Fairytale scene.

He fights off the image, which becomes twisted and distorted. He puts down his weapon and rubs his eyes.

Jusuf as the Old Carpenter disappears for a moment. The Fairytale scene continues to flicker.

Vladimir sights again. But the Muslim sniper is gone. The doors of the church slam closed and there is a deep silence.

Vladimir comes out from his hiding place and walks up to the dead bodies of the old people. With his foot, he rolls over one of the old women. Her eyes are open and fixed. Her face is twisted into a mask of horror. Vladimir turns pale at the sight and tries to hide.

Vladimir crumples into a corner of the church building behind a bush. The lights flicker, and the church people remove the bodies. The Fairytale

people start to appear again. The Old Carpenter
(Jusuf) and his Wife fade into Vladimir's view.

Jusuf is sitting on his cot in his shelter, and he
too goes into the Fairytale. He sees himself as the Old
Carpenter, and he sees his Wife.

Then one
day an Old
Carpenter and his
Wife are looking into
their bags of 'warm
fuzzies.' They have
been married for
many years but have
not been able to have children. However, they long
for a baby and dream of nothing else.

The Old Carpenter puts on his nightshirt and
climbs into bed. His Wife is brushing her hair.

The Old Carpenter says, "Wouldn't it be
wonderful to have a child? What if we give each other
love this time? I have two 'fuzzies' left and it will give
me great joy to give one to you this night."

The face of his Wife is aglow with a wonderful
Love-Light. She says, "My husband, I have three
'fuzzies' left, and it will make me most happy to share
one with you this night. And if we have a child, I will
have one to share with it and one to give
to St. Peter when I die."

She comes to bed and they
embrace tenderly.

The Old Carpenter whispers, "I
love you, my wife."

The Wife whispers back, "And I

love you too, my husband."

Their bags shrink and a little magic sparkles and sprinkles out around them.

The Fairytale scene changes, the colors become brighter and a beautiful handmade cradle appears. The Wife is in labor.

So it comes to pass that a baby girl is born to the Old Carpenter and his Wife. It is the first love

baby since the Wicked Witch had cast her spell, and there in her cradle is a bag stuffed full of 'warm fuzzies.' The Old Carpenter and his Wife marvel at this, but decide to tell no one.

The lights flicker in both Jusuf and Vladimir's mind and the Fairytale scene and Fairytale people slowly disappear.

As Jusuf comes out of the Fairytale, joy fills his face, and he is smiling. He mumbles to himself... "I'm a father. I'm a FATHER!" It is as if he is still in the Fairytale. He spins around and shouts at the top of his lungs. "I know a secret! Vladimir! Where ever you are! I love you my friend! I love everybody!" He dances around the shelter, with his mother watching in amazement.

Vladimir's face is lit up with a broad smile. He stands, looks around and tries to shoot his weapon in the air. It clicks and will not fire. He shouts, "Yes, Yes, YES!"

Wouldn't it be wonderful if soldiers everywhere would run out of bullets?

CHAPTER 24
Medical Supplies

Late that winter, Jusuf goes to Mostar to get medical supplies for the hospital in Konjic. He hiked the mountain trail to scout out all the sniper spots and mark them on his map. While in Mostar, he has had a wonderful place to stay, with old friends of his father. He even was able to sleep in a real bed last night. Today, he spent most of the day packing and repacking the backpack he would carry through the mountains.

Tonight, Jusuf is climbing up the steep and narrow mountain trail, from Mostar to Konjic. He is carrying the large backpack. The way is treacherous during the day, but doubly so at night even though there is a full moon.

Right now, a CNN news correspondent is following him, carrying a small video camera. The correspondent sniffed Jusuf out at the hospital and could smell a very important story. Since then he has stuck to Jusuf like glue.

The correspondent is trying to shoot video footage as they move up the trail. At this point, the trail is a little wider, and he would like to get in front of Jusuf and get the shot of him coming up the trail. But try as he may, the best he can do is get up even with him and get a side shot.

Jusuf is one-hundred percent focused on the task at hand.

The correspondent falls in behind him and asks, "Why are you carrying the medical supplies over such a dangerous trail?"

Jusuf responds without looking back, "The roads have been blocked for months, and the hospital in Konjic has nothing to work with. This trail is watched during the day, so I'll try and slip through tonight."

The correspondent asks, "Were you able to get food in Mostar?"

Jusuf says, "I ate my best meal all year before I left."

"I meant, were you able to bring food back?"

Jusuf laughs, "I have forty kilos of medical supplies, which is all I can carry. There's no room for food."

The correspondent is shocked, "Forty kilos!" He is panting heavily, 'Do you think we can take a break, so I can get more than a butt shot of you?"

Jusuf explains, "I have to hike sixty kilometers through the mountains, and I have only eight hours of darkness to do it in. I don't have time for breaks, but when we get to Konjic you can take all the footage you want."

Suddenly they come under fire. Someone is shooting at the sound of their voices or their shadows in the trees.

The correspondent ducks for cover, but struggles to keep filming the gun flashes, but as he looks up the trail... Jusuf picks up his pace as he races into the darkness.

The correspondent turns the camera on himself and speaks softly, "He can't be more than fifteen, and he's carrying over eighty pounds, and I can't keep up! He is a true hero in this war!"

The lights flash in Jusuf's mind and the  Fairytale scene and Fairytale people start to appear. A Little Girl appears. While running Jusuf goes into the Fairytale, but it does not stop him or slow him down. On the contrary, it seems to give him superhuman strength and the nimbleness of a deer.

Jusuf races up the trail, leaping from stone to stone in the darkness. He lengthens his stride going down a short but steep grade, letting his weight and the pack's weight propel him forward. When he faces the next sharp incline, he attacks it with short choppy running steps right to the top of that grade. When we can't see him, we can hear his breathing. It is a slow even powerful exhale followed by a relaxed deep inhale. It sounds like an elk stag flying through the open woods at top speed.

As the years pass the Little Girl grows strong and straight. She can always remember the love from the "warm fuzzy" her mother had given her, but as kind as her father always is to her, she can never feel that he loves her.

As Jusuf runs up the mountain, his face is streaming with tears and perspiration. The Fairytale scene and Fairytale people fade out of his mind.

As he comes out of the Fairytale, for a moment, he sees the face of his own father and he remembers the moments they spent in the shop together. He remembers his love and gentle care. He remembers his sound advice and wise view of life.

Jusuf finally tops the mountain overlooking Konjic and looks down. He pauses for a few seconds taking in the beautiful panorama.

He pulls on the straps of the pack to tighten them and plunges down the steep trail, jumping from stone to stone, foothold to foothold. All the time, he is acutely aware of any eminent danger. As he crosses a mountain road, he can see a Serbian bunker about fifty meters away. The posted guard is asleep at his post. Jusuf passes quickly without being noticed.

Soon he comes down onto a dirt road. Jusuf freezes in his tracks and stares into the darkness. His eyes are so accustom to the darkness, he can see a shadowy image of a car sitting on the road. He watches and waits. After a very long minute the headlights on the car flash, three short, three long, three short. That's the signal.

The car is sitting on the side of the dirt road, about a hundred meters away. The lights flash once more, and Jusuf runs for the car. The driver turns the car around, gets out and opens the trunk. When Jusuf reaches him, he helps him off with the heavy pack, which is almost too heavy for him, and puts it in the trunk. They both jump in the car and it speeds down the road toward the village.

The driver quickly reaches a speed that is frightening to Jusuf.

Jusuf is holding on with white knuckles, "150 kilometers an hour! Why so fast?"

"To avoid being hit by sniper fire."

As Jusuf leans his head back to relax, his mind flashes back to a time with his father eight years earlier. He pictures his father as he labored over a woodcarving. Jusuf was barely able to see the top of the bench. His father reached down and picked him up and put him on his knee. Then he went back to work, with his arms around him. Jusuf could now see his father's hands as he skillfully chiseled at the carving. He concentrated on every move as the figure emerged magically from the wood.

The driver glances at Jusuf's concentrated face. "You all right?"

Jusuf responds slowly, "I'm fine, just a little tired. I was thinking about my father."

The driver comments, "You have a right to be tired, and your father would be proud of you."

A platoon of Croatian militia is moving along from one protective point to another. They can hear the car coming down the street and get ready to fire on the car. They point their weapons directly at the road, where the car has to pass.

As the car speeds through the village, they shoot wildly at the difficult target. Most of the militia fire when the car is passing, which is too late. The car takes a couple of hits, one ricocheting off the back window and another bouncing off the back bumper. Most of the bullets ricochet off the road and surrounding buildings. Their attempt is more comical than critical, with the bullets bouncing back at them. They end up doing a strange dodging dance to avoid their own bullets.

CHAPTER 25
War Without Enemies

The driver and Jusuf quickly speed down the street and out of site.

Unfortunately for the platoon, their leader doesn't see the humor of their antics.

Their leader, Ante, shouts at his men, "You stupid bastards! You're wasting ammo. I've never seen such lousy shots. My blind dog is a better shot standing on three legs and taking a piss. Now get in your positions and stand ready.

The platoon takes various positions in amongst the houses. Fortunately, they are in a total state of unpreparedness. Ante stands studying there confusion; shaking his head.

Aisha comes walking up the street on her way to the hospital. She is about to pass the platoon, when she sees the militia leader and stops.

She recognizes him and waves, "Yoo-hoo, Ante. Is that you, Ante?"

Ante spins around with his gun at the ready position.

Aisha casually moves up closer to meet him. When he recognizes her, he puts up his weapon.

Ante smiles and greats her, "Aisha, I didn't recognize you in that nurse's uniform."

Aisha pats him on arm, "How are you, Ante?"

Ante standing proudly, "I'm just fine. How are you?"

Aisha makes light of her situation, "Things are hard, but we manage. How is your lovely wife,

Marina, and the children? I haven't seen them in some time now."

Ante looks down sadly, "I sent them to Germany to be with my cousin about six months ago."

Aisha is shocked, "I hope you haven't had a quarrel. You're such a grand couple, and you're such a fine father."

Ante says, "No, it's 'cause of the war. I sure miss'em!"

Aisha says, "You should go to them. You're too good a man to be involved in all this fighting and killing. But I understand, because Meho has been away since the fighting started, but he will be home soon, I hope."

Ante is puzzled, "I was sorry to hear about... Meho..." He catches himself, looks around and changes the subject. "You know, you shouldn't be on the streets? It isn't safe."

Aisha says, "Oh hooey, you don't need to worry. I'm going to the hospital to help with the sick and wounded, and at this hour of the morning there isn't any traffic."

Ante responds looking at his men, "I'm not worried about the traffic."

She looks at him strangely, not understanding, then shrugs it off, and says, "Why don't you stop by for dinner? We don't have much, but there is always enough for an extra plate."

Ante responds genuinely, "Thank you! Maybe I'll do that."

She gives him a big hug and turns to leave, "Take care now, you hear."

Ante waves her off, "You too. Bye for now."

Aisha turns and starts to walk up the street.

Ante is dumbfounded, and shakes his head.

Suddenly she draws fire from the platoon. She is totally unaware.

Ante runs after her shouting at his men, "Cease fire! CEASE FIRE, DAMN IT!

He steps behind Aisha, back to back, and walks backwards to keep up with her. He shoots over the heads of his men, until they stop shooting.

Ante shouts back at them, "She's my laundry woman! Thank God you can't hit the broad side of a barn!"

The men in the platoon look at each other curiously.

Aisha looks back at Ante, who turns and tips his hat as she smiles and walks away.

The smile is contagious as Ante turns back to his men. He looks at them and says, "What the hell am I doing here?"

CHAPTER 26
Harsh Reality of War

Aisha and Jusuf are sound asleep in their shelter. It is shortly after midnight, the night of Kurban Bajram, a Muslim high holy day.

There is a violent storm raging. The rain beats down on the bulkhead of the shelter, creating a loud drumming sound, and drowning out all other sound. Thus, it is lulling Aisha and Jusuf into a false sense of security.

A number of military vehicles are coming down the street. They pull up in front of the shelter. It is the Serbian militia led by Ranko and Vladimir. Ranko jumps from the lead jeep, with his .45 at the ready. Vladimir and his platoon jump from the next trucks. The other platoon disembarks from the last trucks, and they all take up positions around the entrance of the shelter The show of force is overwhelming!

Ranko shouts over the storm, "Break in the door and drag the garbage out here."

Vladimir motions to his men. They throw open the cellar bulkhead ripping it from its hinges, and then they start to kick down the door.

Aisha and Jusuf are startled out of their sleep. Jusuf rushes to the door to reinforce it. Aisha begins to scream inside the shelter.

Jusuf braces himself against the door, shouting, "What are you trying to do? We have done nothing."

Vladimir's face remains fixed and stern.

The two boys lean against the door each trying to out power the other. Finally, the door gives way and Jusuf falls to the floor with Vladimir on top of the door and him. Vladimir's men help him up, while the others throw the door aside, grab Jusuf and Aisha, and drag them up the steps in their nightclothes. They throw them to the muddy ground in front of Ranko. Jusuf looks up at Vladimir, with fear and confusion in his eyes.

All they can do is stare at each other. Finally, Vladimir motions for Jusuf to be calm. This does not help Jusuf's confusion.

Ranko steps forward deliberately presses his foot on Aisha's hand and grinds it into the mud. She winces in pain.

Ranko snarls, "You can be taken to a detention camp, where you'll get proper food and shelter, or be cleansed from this area."

Aisha looks up at him, "What do you mean? This is our home!"

Ranko spits back, "I'd prefer the cleansing, but you got a choice, because of Vladimir's intervention." Ranko presses his foot harder on her hand.

Aisha screams out, "O.K., O.K.! We'll go!"

Jusuf struggles against those restraining him. He shouts, "No, Mama! I've heard about your proper food and shelter. I would rather die here and now." He looks Vladimir in the eye, and screams, "If you were ever my friend, you would kill me now. Shoot me! SHOOT!"

Aisha says to Vladimir, "My son has gone slightly mad, from the hardships of the war. Of course we will be happy to accept your kind offer."

Ranko, motions to an aid, who brings a document clipboard and holds an umbrella over it. Then Ranko turns to Aisha.

He says cruelly, "First, you must sign over the rights to your land to my command."

Vladimir is shocked at what his father is trying to do. "This is not part of our agreement!"

Aisha stares into Ranko's eyes. Her mind flashes back to when she was only fourteen. She can see it happening all over again. She is being raped by her family's Serbian landlord. He threatens to kill her and strikes her across the face. Then she sees the landlord beating her father with a bullwhip. His son is restraining her, and she screams, "Papa. Papa!" The tears stream down her face.

Aisha repeats intensely, but softly, "Papa! Papa!"

Then Aisha's face floods with anger, which quickly boils into rage. In a moment of complete sanity... She stands and spits in Ranko's face.

Ranko goes crazy. He draws a bayonet, grabs her by the hair and puts the knife to her throat.

Ranko snarls, "You'll sign and then I will cut your garbage throat, bitch."

Vladimir steps behind his father and grabs his knife hand. He twists his hand away from Aisha and frees her. They struggle with the knife between them.

Jusuf pulls his mother to safety, and turns to see it is not going well for Vladimir. He is terrified that his friend will be killed. He takes up the clipboard and signs it.

Jusuf shouts to Ranko, "There I've signed. I've signed! Stop! Don't hurt him! Let us go!"

Vladimir gets the knife, but Ranko draws his .45 and points it at Vladimir.

Ranko shouts, "Step back!"

Vladimir steps back, still holding the knife pointed Ranko.

Ranko points the gun at Aisha, "Sign, bitch! Sign it!"

When he looks back at Vladimir, Vladimir is holding his rifle at his hip pointed directly at him.

Vladimir's eyes are cold, his jaw fixed. Their eyes lock in a deadly stare.

Ranko has seen this killing expression before, raises the .45, and points it between Vladimir's eyes.

Vladimir considers his options. He knows his father's cruelty and drops the knife.

Ranko turns to his men, "Load the garbage on the truck."

Vladimir walks over to Aisha and puts his poncho around her. He helps her on to a truck. As he turns back, he looks for Jusuf.

Jusuf is being forced toward another truck. When Jusuf looks back at his friend, his face softens, and he says, "Thank you."

Vladimir just nods.

Two soldiers force Jusuf onto the truck.

CHAPTER 27
Hope Eternal

The real world, in which the Boys now live, has broken them completely apart. They have no hope of ever seeing each other again.

Here, in a large detention shed for men (or a concentration camp might be more appropriate), Jusuf is sitting on the floor in the corner away from the other inmates. There are not enough beds, and many men are sleeping on the floor. Jusuf notices an old man who has five other prisoners sleeping around him on the floor.

By the only entrance, two guards keep watch.

Back in Konjic, Vladimir is sleeping in his own bedroom. He is tossing and turning in his sleep, tortured by thoughts that he made the wrong decision to send Jusuf to the detention camp, where he wouldn't starve to death or have the guards kill him. Suddenly, he wakes with a start, sits straight up in bed and rubs his eyes.

 The only world that connects the Boys now is the Fairytale, which they both experience at the same time.

The lights flash in the minds of both Vladimir and Jusuf. The Fairytale scene starts to appear. The Old Carpenter's Wife is in bed, and the Little Girl is sitting by her side. Jusuf goes into the Fairytale as the Old Carpenter and stands by the door watching them with great interest.

In the Fairytale that winter, when the darkness is the heaviest over the land, the Little Girl's mother takes ill, and it seems that she is going to die. The Little Girl and her father stay with her all day and into the night. As the Little Girl cares for  her, she gives her mother one 'warm fuzzy' after another. The Old Carpenter marvels at what she is doing, but every time he starts to warn her, he notices that his wife is getting stronger from the 'warm fuzzies.' So the Little Girl just gives and gives until she becomes so tired that she falls asleep with her head on her mother's bed.

The Old Carpenter walks in and stands next to the bed. He gently strokes his daughter's hair.

Finally, his Wife opens her eyes, and the Old Carpenter takes her hand. Love and joy light up his face, but just when he is about to speak, she reaches up and puts her fingers to his lips.

The Wife says, "You don't need to say it. I know what's in your heart. Save your last 'fuzzy'!" She strokes her daughter's hair.

The Old Carpenter blurts out, "She has worked so hard to make you well again, and I'm afraid that she has given you most of her 'fuzzies'."

"Oh, my husband, she is so young. She will need them to find a good man and maybe have love children of her own. You must tell her, so she can count them out."

The Old Carpenter hangs his head sadly saying, "You are right, my wife. I wish I had more for her and for you."

Just then, the Little Girl wakes up. When she sees that her mother is well again, she smiles and the light on her face lights up the room. She throws her arms about her mother's neck and kisses her on both cheeks. When she reaches into her bag, to takes out a 'warm fuzzy' and give it to her, her father reaches out and gently takes her hand to stop her.

He smiles kindly at her, and says, "I know that you love your mother very much, but there is something that you should know. When all your 'warm fuzzies' are gone you shall get no more, for the magic left the village when I was just a boy. You must save what you have left to give to your husband and your children. The last one you must save until you die to give to St. Peter to show your love for God.

The Little Girl looks in her bag, then looks in her hand. A tear comes to her eye as she looks into her father's gentle face. She says, "It is my last one, Papa."

The Old Carpenter slumps into the chair next to the bed, with his head in his hands. He cries out, "Oh God, forgive me! What have I done?"

For the first time since the Little Girl can remember, she sees her father start to cry. The Little Girl goes to her father and tries to put her arms around him to comfort him, but his grief is very great. Then suddenly she takes the "warm fuzzy" that is in her hand and presses it in close to his heart.

The Little Girl says, "St. Peter will just have to understand. Papa, I love you very much."

The Old Carpenter looks up into his daughter's innocent face. His heart is about to burst. Finally, he can hold back no longer, and he takes his daughter into his arms, saying, "And I love you, my dearest daughter!"

His bag shrinks and falls limp at his waist. Alas, it is empty.

His Wife gasps, "My husband!" She holds her hand over her mouth.

Slowly the Old Carpenter looks into his bag. He then looks at his wife and smiles, saying, "Well, St. Peter will just have to understand."

The Little Girl suddenly realizes why her father has never said this before. She hugs him tightly, exclaiming, "That was your last one, too!"

The Wife holds out her arms and says to them, "Come here, the both of you."

She embraces them both at the same time, saying, "I love you both, with all the love that's in me. So there, now all our bags are empty."

Just then, the cock crows three times and the morning sun thunders through the window. Like magic, all their bags pop full again. As the Wife looks into her bag to check it for the last time, her mouth falls open in astonishment.

She holds it up to the others, "My bag is full."

The Old Carpenter and Little Girl quickly open their bags.

The Old Carpenter says, "And so is mine!"

The Little Girl smiles, "And so is mine! But I thought the magic had left the village."

The Old Carpenter ponders for a moment, "So did I..., but then no one ever emptied their bags after the widow woman left the village."

The Wife exclaims, "It doesn't matter, my darling husband. The magic is still with us, and our dearest daughter has helped us find it again. We shall tell everyone in the village today.

But the Old Carpenter asks, "What if they don't believe us, my sweetheart?"

His Wife responds joyously, "Then give them a 'warm fuzzy' or two. That should shock them a bit. When they see that we never run out, they might get the idea."

The Little Girl makes a pledge, "I shall empty my bag every day and never count how many 'warm fuzzies' I give away."

The Fairytale scene fades from the minds of Vladimir and Jusuf along with the Fairytale people, including Jusuf's Old Carpenter.

Jusuf jumps for joy and begins to rush about shouting. "Yes. Yes. Yes! The love of Allah is with us! Allah be Praised!"

The guards move among the others handing out food.

The others in the detention shed turn to look at Jusuf. His face is radiant.

A guard shoves a bowl of gruel into his chest, and says, "There, get excited over that, because you won't get any more for three days."

The old man asks the guard, "Some for me! For the love of Allah? You gave me nothing yesterday."

Another guard kicks the old man to the floor, shouting, "I'll give you the love of Allah! You're a blue tag. You're not gonna get anything for two more days. And if you "Allah" me again tomorrow, I'll cut your rations again, just like I did yesterday. You understand, old man?"

When the guards turn away, Jusuf kneels to the starving old man and gives him his bowl.

The old man hesitates, "I cannot take your food. You shall have nothing more for three days."

Jusuf is still bubbling with joy, "You must, I insist. The love of Allah is with us!"

The old man whispers, "Allah be Praised!" He takes the food and digs in.

Vladimir's reaction to the Fairytale is quite different. What he has seen here is a total contradiction of what his father has been telling him. His conscious awareness keeps asking, "What is the truth?"

Vladimir begins a long slow scream, "NOOOOOOO!" He pounds his head, with his fists.

Ranko burst in the room, with a .45 pistol at the ready. He points it in all directions around the room, but sees nothing. He slowly lowers the gun and asks, "What's the problem?"

Vladimir responds timidly, "I was having a nightmare."

Ana stands in the doorway and listens without being noticed.

Ranko is stern and gives him no sympathy. "Nightmares are a sign of weakness."

Ana goes to Vladimir and takes him in her arms. She tries to comfort him, "It's O.K.! It's okay." She turns to Ranko, and says, "You must have forgotten everything you learned in psychology. Vladimir's nightmares are your fault. He is only a boy, and what you have put him through would give anybody with a conscience a nightmare."

Ranko goes into a rage. He starts shouting at Ana. "You stupid slut! Who do you think you're talking to?" Then he slaps her across the face, sending her flying to the floor. "You're just my whore! Don't ever question my knowledge or judgment! As for Vladimir, he is my son. He will do what I tell him to do. And so will you! I am in command here." With that, he kicks her and stomps out the door.

Vladimir goes to his mother, helps her to her feet and gives her a hug. Shocked by his father's behavior, he tries to minimize it, "He really didn't mean all those things."

Ana, with tears in her eyes, touches her son's cheek tenderly. She stands and starts to leave. She pauses in the doorway before turning back. She says in a very matter-of-fact tone, "You really don't know your father." With a knowing nod, she turns and leaves.

Vladimir looks after her. An expression of realization begins to fill his face.

CHAPTER 28
Transformations

No matter where you are, no matter how difficult your circumstances, no matter how gloomy the people are around you, Mother Nature will always transform the autumn season with rich and vibrant colors. It is such a morning, when Jusuf comes out of the detention shed and kneels in morning prayer.

The guards turn and watch him carefully.

One guard says to the other, "Look, the heathen's going to pray. Hey, kid, I'd be happy to shove your face in the dirt." He laughs at what he thinks is a very clever comment.

The other guard builds on the insult with maniacal laughter, "You want me to ventilate your skull. Be easier for Allah to get in."

The two guards laugh boisterously at their own cleverness.

One by one, the other prisoners, take courage from Jusuf, and join him in morning prayers. As their number grows, the guards become more insulting and laugh hysterically at their own humor.

One guard says, "Look at that? A flock of pecking birds."

The other guard chimes in, "Well I'm going to send the little bastard to his maker." He raises his rifle to shoot Jusuf.

Fortunately, at that moment a Red Cross jeep pulls up to the gate.

The first guard taps the second guard on the shoulder and points out the jeep. The second guard quickly lowers his rifle and tries to look nonchalant. The guards then force Jusuf and the prisoners back into their detention shed area.

That same beautiful fall morning, Vladimir is standing on the front porch of the Rakic estate looking up into the hills. His outward gaze reveals an inward struggle. Then as though remembering an ancient religious ritual, he clasps his hands and bows his head in prayer.

"Oh, Lord, show me what I must do and give me the strength and courage to do it."

At that moment, a ray of sunlight pierces through the trees and strikes his chest. It slowly slides up to his face, and as Vladimir lifts his head he closes his eyes and his features soften with the intense light.

At the same moment, a beam of sunlight comes through the window of the detention shed and lights up Jusuf's face in the same manner. With a feeling of submission, they allow themselves to go into the Fairytale.

 The lights flash in their minds, the Fairytale scene and village people appear. Jusuf appears as the Old Carpenter and Vladimir appears as the Young Prince.

So it is in the small village. It doesn't happen overnight, but little by little people learn that the magic isn't gone after all and they begin to empty their bags. Then in the morning they are full of "warm fuzzies" again. Before long, there are more love babies and new bags to empty every day.

One day while the Old Carpenter is putting a new roof on a house, the Young Prince rides by dressed in his fine clothes. The Old Carpenter turns to the Young Prince and gives him a "warm fuzzy" in the old long-forgotten manner... "I will always be your friend no matter what."

The Young Prince looks up to the Old Carpenter and says, "You best be careful how you give 'fuzzies' away."

The Old Carpenter smiles and laughs, "My bag is filled every morning. Can I give you a handful to help you through the day?"

The Young Prince is cautious, "I don't believe you. You're trying to trick me."

The Old Carpenter says kindly, "How far have we come that you can't trust me?"

The Young Prince was the hardest to convince.

In the Fairytale, Jusuf turns to watch Vladimir as he rides away. He can feel the doubt and confusion that he is going through. He reaches into his bag, takes out a handful of "warm fuzzies" and blows them after his friend. The "fuzzies" sparkle through the air and enter the Prince's bag. It pops plump again.

The Young Prince rides his horse through the beautiful autumn forest painted in all its glorious colors. A new peacefulness comes into his body and he sits taller and straighter in his saddle. Soon he approaches the castle and the Princess comes out to greet him.

Now his Princess finds ways he can't resist. When he comes home tired and beaten, she bathes him, rubs his sore muscles with oil and then makes love to him. She shows him so much affection that one night she empties her bag and can give no more.

The Young Prince says to himself, "Aha! She has used her last and now she shall have no more."

But when morning comes and he peeks into her bag, to his astonishment it is stuffed full. All he can do is scratch his head in puzzlement. When he looks in his own bag, he can't help but wonder where the extra "fuzzies" came from.

As Vladimir walks about his house, he comes out of the Fairytale. The Fairytale people disappear. The Fairytale scene lingers in his mind. Then he reacts on himself as he is scratching his head. He turns to look at himself in the mirror.

When he sees his reflection, it is as if he is looking in a pool of water, and he notices that he is covered in "warm fuzzy" dust. He smiles as a yellow and red leaf falls into the small pool into which he is looking. Startled, he looks around. Vladimir suddenly finds that he is standing at a pool on the estate high up in the hills.

He says to himself, confidently, "Of course!"

CHAPTER 29
Truth Be Known

In the mountains around Konjic, winter sets in. Snow covers the mountaintops. But when the sun breaks through the gray clouds, the beauty is spectacular, and it lifts the spirits of everyone.

Nedjo is sitting in his reading chair. He is wearing his seeing device and reading the newspaper. As he reads, there is an occasional audible reaction, "Aha... Woe, wee... Yaws a!" He punctuates these phrases with the repeated, "You got that right!" When he finishes the paper, he sets it down, smiles and ponders how all this is going to play out.

Vladimir is on the move. His gradual change is taking root. Every day he visits all three platoons of Serbian soldiers in his area. In one platoon, he questions the soldiers about the truthfulness of their commanding officers. In another platoon he questions the reasons behind their orders to kill innocent people, some of who are their friends. In the third platoon, he questions who is going to profit from their killing and being killed.

Vladimir keeps coming in and out of the  Fairytale scene, first seeing himself as the Young Prince character, then switching back to himself in real life. Because all this relates to the Fairytale, Nedjo is able to watch Vladimir's transformation as he switches from the Young Prince back to himself and moves quickly from group to group.

In the Fairytale, the Young Prince is soon the best of all. Some say that he travels the world so fast and so many times that he can empty his bag three times in twenty-four hours. At this point Vladimir's life begins to 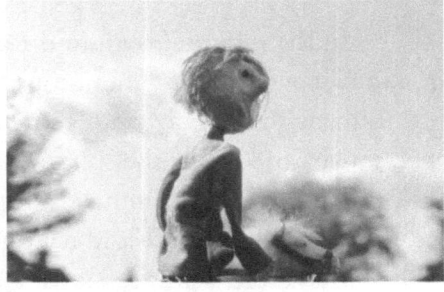 parallel that of the Young Prince so closely that you can hardly tell them apart. He is becoming the person he was always meant to be.

Finally, Vladimir climbs the mountain to see Nedjo. He has many questions, and he knows that his friend Nedjo is more than glad to help him work on them.

They talk about the war and the things that are happening in the Fairytale. Nedjo makes it clear that Vladimir has to decide for himself what to do. But he says, "I will give you the facts about the war, so you can see the truth and make the right decisions."

Nedjo shows him newspaper clippings of the attempts at a negotiated peace, and the frustration of the UN peacekeeping forces. He shows him video tapes of CNN news broadcasts about the peace negotiations and the war. One of the clips is Jusuf's mountain trek.

This is all new to Vladimir. He begins to realize that he has been deceived.

Nedjo shows him tapes of what is being broadcast on Belgrade TV. Vladimir is shocked by the lies.

Nedjo shows him a huge stack of letters, "These are from small community leaders from all over Yugoslavia. They all say the same thing. They don't like the ethnic division, the false peace of the military and self-appointed politicians, or the killing and destruction. They all want to know how to stop it and who to turn to. They all feel that the rest of the world doesn't care what happens to them."

Vladimir takes this information and makes another tour of the soldiers in the Serbian platoons. He makes every attempt to stop the fighting. At a mortar position, he approaches his old platoon.

Vladimir calls out with a sense of urgency, "Cease fire! The politicians have signed a cease fire agreement at the peace negotiations!"

One soldier is shocked, "You're kidding!"

Another says, "We've heard nothing of the sort. In fact Belgrade TV says different."

Yet another asks, "Can't we just keep fighting? I don't have a job to go back to."

Vladimir is emphatic, "An order is an order. If you keep killing, you are not protected under the rules of war. You can be charged with murder."

Vladimir takes his next opportunity to visit some of his Serbian compatriots from another platoon. He uses that occasion to engage in an argument with the other soldiers in their makeshift barracks.

Vladimir asks, "What's to be gained by more killing?"

One Serb says, "We want more territory."

Another Serb says, "Protected access to Belgrade."

A third Serb says, "A Greater Serbia."

The first Serb comes back with, "To cleanse the land of Muslims and Croatians."

Vladimir seizes this opportunity to make his point, "How's your new society going to function? In 1981 only 19% of the population was Serbian. If you kill off 81 % of the people or drive them away, who will be left to make the community work? Who will bake the bread? Do you know any Serbian bakers in Konjic? Who will work the farms? Does anyone know any Serbian farmers, not land owners, farmers who know how to work the land? Who will fix your shoes? Do you know any Serbian cobblers?" He grabs up a chair a soldier is sitting on and smashes it into little bits. "There! Is there anyone here that can put it back together again, or make a new one?"

The men are now silent.

Vladimir drives his point home, "No, there were only two in all of Konjic that could fix it or make a new one, and one has been killed and the other has been driven away and is probably dead by now. So what do we do? We now have one chair less. If we keep up this insanity we soon won't have anything to sit on." He pulls an ammunition crate out from under one of the soldiers and holds it up. "Except maybe these ammo crates and that is your Greater Serbia."

The men sit or stand staring at the ammo crate. Their countenance falls. They can no longer hide behind platitudes, slogans or propaganda.

The next day, Vladimir goes into high gear. He races from group to group. It looks like a repeat of the Young Prince's race around his known world.

Vladimir carries a meager edition of the Sarajevo newspaper. It is only four pages, but the fact that it even exists is a credit to the dedicated journalists, who believe that reporting news is as important as food itself. The banner headline reads, BORGA JE ZAVRSHENA, which means "THE FIGHTING IS OVER." The men stop their shelling, and Vladimir runs on to the next position and the next.

In the Fairytale, the Young Prince seems to take on superhuman strength. His gallant steed gallops so fast he seems to take on wings. The Young Prince wears no armor. He carries no weapon of any kind. He carries only the truth and a bag of "warm fuzzies."

CHAPTER 30
Confrontation

At the command center in Konjic, Ranko is checking the ropes on a Croatian woman lying over a coffee table. Her hands and feet are bound, and she is blindfolded and gagged. Her clothes are already partially torn away, exposing her bare breasts and pubic area. Ranko has been, you might say, "interrogating" the female Croatian prisoner.

As you can imagine, Vladimir's actions do not go unnoticed. It does not take long before Ranko has sent for Vladimir to report to him at his Konjic command center.

When Vladimir enters the command center, he is smiling, but when he surveys the situation, his mood changes from joy to disgust.

Ranko attacks from the outset, "Shit, Vladimir, what have you been doing? I'm getting bombarded by reports that you've told the men to stop fighting."

Vladimir immediately goes on the offence, "Why are you lying to the men? The Serbs have signed a peace agreement, yet we keep fighting. Have you seen the paper? Or don't you read?"

Vladimir throws the newspaper at him.

Ranko tears it up, without looking at it. He is in Vladimir's face in a nanosecond, shouting, "This is my command, you bastard. The fighting isn't over 'till I say it's over! Stop this crusade, or I'll have your stripes!"

Vladimir is frozen by his father's attack.

Ranko steps next to the Croatian woman, saying, "Demonstrate your loyalty to me and to my command." He holds out his pistol, "Take my pistol! Go on take it!" He shouts, "I order you to kill that Croatian garbage!"

The woman starts to scream through the gag and struggles against the ropes.

Vladimir looks at the woman and then back at his father, saying, "You are one sick bastard!"

With that, he tears off his stripes, throws them in his father's face, turns and walks away.

Ranko shouts after him, "Come back here! I said come back! I order you to come back here!"

Ranko aims the pistol at his back, but Vladimir steps out the door and out of sight. Ranko turns and shoots the woman in the head repeatedly.

CHAPTER 31
Facing Opposition

At Serbian Command Headquarters in Sarajevo, the room is filled with smoke, and a bottle of Jack Daniel's is sitting on the corner of the desk. Ranko is sitting across from Jovanovic, who is sitting at his desk. His office is large and tastelessly decadent. The priceless Victorian desk, at which they sit, has been painted in camouflage colors. Both men are smoking cigars. Both men are laughing hysterically.

General Jovancvic says, "You should have seen the chairman's face. He was so relieved; he actually thanked me for my support. He actually believes that we are the only ones who are honoring the peace agreement."

Ranko, blows a smoke ring, "It sounds like you have them eating out of your hand."

Jovanovic says, "I'm telling you, the UN will give us everything we want. All we have to do is keep up the ruse a little longer."

Ranko asks, "So what do we do about Vladimir. Right now, he's a loose cannon."

"So far, I have gotten a lot of millage out of his antics. He has actually played right into my hands. With the committee, I held him up as a symbol of our sincerity. Now we need to see how pliable he can be. Have you said anything to him about this meeting?"

"No, nor has he said anything to me"

"Good, I am determined to see if I can get any more mileage out of Vladimir's one-man crusade. Are we in agreement?"

"Affirmative. I'm sure he'll listen to you."

Jovanovic presses the button on the intercom, and says, "Tell the guard to send Vladimir in."

Vladimir enters and walks briskly to the front of the desk. He comes to attention saluting the General, who casually returns the salute, but does not tell him to stand at ease.

Vladimir barks out, "Private Rakic reporting, Sir."

Being fully briefed, Jovanovic does not react to his rank of Private. He moves slowly around the desk until he is standing next to the boy.

Jovanovic says without emotion, "Because of your grandfather and father, you've a future in the military, boy. If you weren't a Rakic, I wouldn't have time for you."

Vladimir does not respond. Jovanovic puts his arm around his shoulder.

Jovanovic puts on a friendly air, "O.K., enough said. Who's been filling your head with these lies you're telling the men?"

Vladimir fires back, "I saw it in the newspaper, SIR."

Jovanovic asks matter-of-factly, "Do you believe everything you read in the papers?

Vladimir does not respond. Jovanovic starts to circle around him.

Jovanovic states, "This is the Serbian position in the peace negotiations. One, we keep the British, Tweedledum and Tweedledee, off balance. Two, we make them believe that the Serbs are truly interested in peace. Three, the longer we can keep them thinking that; the longer they will continue to enforce the arms embargo against the Bosnians. Four, the longer the peace negotiations carry on the longer we keep the United States out. We got enough friends in U.S. intelligence and the Pentagon to keep Clinton running in circles for years."

Vladimir barks back respectfully, "I had no idea that you had planned such a cunning strategy, SIR."

Jovanovic continues in the same tone, "I'll simplify our goals for you. We take as much territory as possible. We learned from the British and French after World War I, carve it up and claim it as your own. When we sign, we will be everybody's brother to get aid from the U.S. and Europe. They're such suckers they'll throw money at us, all in the name of helping the poor war-ravaged people."

Vladimir responds, avoiding confrontation, "Will the military be the real recipients of the aid, SIR?"

Jovanovic chuckles, "Who else? The military, the government, it's all the same. When it's over, you and your father will be very wealthy. We'll milk 'em for all they're worth, then take the rest of the territory. It'll be the birth of the Greater Serbia. Do you get the idea?

Vladimir confirms, "I understand, SIR. Thank you for taking me into your confidence, SIR."

Jovanovic pats him on the back, saying, "I knew I could count on you. You're dismissed."

Vladimir salutes. Jovanovic returns the salute. Vladimir does an about-face and marches out the door.

Jovanovic turns to Ranko, saying, "Keep an eye on that boy. He was too easy. I would've preferred a little fight. Hell! Maybe we can chalk it up to his youth."

Ranko responds assuring him, "Yea, Vladimir's just easy to lead."

It is obvious that they no longer know Vladimir, and who is manipulating who. As General Eisenhower liked to quote, "Give your enemies enough rope and they'll hang themselves."

CHAPTER 32
The Promise

When the sun rises on this day, it looks just like any other day at the detention camp. Jusuf and many other prisoners are already in morning prayer. But this day is about to become a very important day for many of the prisoners.

There is a group of vehicles on the road, headed for the detention camp. The convoy includes three Red Cross buses and a squad of UN peacekeepers. It is about midday when they pull up outside the compound fence.

A group of male prisoners and guards, including Jusuf and the old man are standing in the men's compound wondering what is going on. Also, a group of female prisoners, including Aisha are standing and watching from the women's compound. The only difference is that the women are lined up and waiting at the gate. They know something the men don't know.

The loudspeakers hiss, crackle and groan as they come on, "Testing, testing, testing." The voice clears his throat. "In compliance to the UN mandate, a number of prisoners will be released as refugees to be assigned to other hosting countries. All the women and children will be released." The loudspeaker clicks off.

The women and children start to board a bus.

The male prisoners are watching in silence as the female prisoners get on the Red Cross buses.

Many of the women wave to their men, and the men wave back.

Aisha searches for Jusuf in the crowd. Finally, she sees him and tries to move toward him.

Aisha calls out, "Meho! Meho!"

The guards move in to stop her. Her face is full of despair, as she is dragged back to the line. Jusuf feels concern and pain for his mother.

He waves timidly, mumbling, "I'm Jusuf, mama!"

The loud speaker comes on again.

The voice announces, "There are not enough places for all the men."

A deep sigh and groan moves through the ranks of the men.

The voice continues, "You will have to draw numbers. Only those getting a number will have a place on the buses."

Guards begin to pass among them with bits of folded paper in their hats. Each man draws out a bit of paper. Some open them at once and immediately show their joy or disappointment. Others hold them tightly in their hands, afraid to face the reality that may be written on them. Jusuf is one of those afraid to open his paper. He looks at Aisha, who is about to get on the bus.

Aisha steps up into the doorway and turns to look back at Jusuf; the question is all over her face. Jusuf unfolds the paper and looks at it. With sadness in his eyes, he looks up to his mother and shakes his head, no. Aisha's mouth falls open and her questioning look turns to fear. The guards prod her to get on the bus.

Jusuf looks down at his blank paper and slowly folds it again, creasing the fold with his fingernails.

Then the old man reaches out and gently takes the bit of paper from him. He then hands him his bit of paper. Jusuf opens it and it has the number 3 on it.

Jusuf is surprised and in awe as he looks at the smiling face of the old man.

He offers the paper back to him, "I cannot accept this."

The old man takes Jusuf's hand and gently closes it about the number. He looks into his eyes, and says, "You have saved me from the wolf, now you must save others. Promise me that you will get strong and come back. Your people need you!"

Jusuf says sincerely, "I promise. May the love of Allah be with you."

Jusuf takes his place in the line of men, number 3, and the men start to board the buses.

The only question now is, in what country they will be accepted as refugees.

CHAPTER 33
Great Debate

In a bombed-out school in Mostar, Vladimir has brought together the Croatian leader and the Muslim leader for a private peace parley. The two leaders are engaged in a heated quarrel over who started the conflict.

The Croatian leader says loudly, "You Muslims started the shelling of our sector."

The Muslim leader responds heatedly, "What?! Croatians started the shelling."

The Croatian leader points his finger, "You're the devil's own liar!"

The Muslim leader snarls, "And you wouldn't know the truth if it bit you on the ass."

The Croatian leader throws up his arms, "Why the hell am I wasting my time here?"

Vladimir tries to intercede, "I brought you together because I always respected you as my teachers in Konjic. You always showed such wisdom and insight. Whatever happened to that?"

The men mumble, but calm down and listen to Vladimir.

Vladimir continues, "Didn't it ever occur to you that neither the Croatians nor the Muslims started the shelling?"

The two men look at each other dumbfounded.

The Muslim leader asks, "What, in Allah's name, are you trying to say?"

Vladimir explains, "I know for a fact that it was my father, who ordered the shelling to get you fighting each other. But that's the past, what's important is what you do now."

The Croatian leader is not convinced, "O.K., but we're forced to fight for more land or lose in the peace negotiations."

Vladimir interjects, "That's more propaganda spread by Jovanovic. It is exactly what he wants you to do. He is making you buy into the old peace treaty of WWI. The UN will not let it go that way. If the two of you can band together you will be able to expose the devil for the liar he is and win over the peace talks."

The Muslim leader says, "I'm not surprised Ranko and General Jovanovic have started all this."

The Croatian leader is still not convinced, "Yea! How do we know we can trust you, Vladimir? Maybe you're setting us up."

The Muslim leader agreed, "Jovanovic was only a puppet of your grandfather. He may be dead, but his ideas are still pulling Jovanovic's strings."

The Croatian leader agrees, "And your father has no conscience either, to maneuver us into this mess."

Vladimir points out with a smile, "Well at least I got you to agree about something. But the fact is I am the only one you **can** trust in all this."

The Croatian leader returns to the same old note from the beginning, "But, now if we don't fight, the village will go to the Muslims."

The Muslim leader snaps back, "The Muslims won't give you one millimeter."

Vladimir says calmly, "Don't start that again. You can live together; just like you always have. The killing has to stop. You can kill me, if that will bring you together."

The two leaders reflect and soften their attitudes slightly.

The Croatian leader surprised, "The devil be damned! You mean that."

Vladimir tries to teach his teachers, "Whatever happened to democracy? Mostar is like Konjic. Serbs, Croats and Muslims have lived together for hundreds of years. Why can't you go to the peace negotiations and insist that you will only accept a democratic solution? Take the power away from the military and the politicians, and return it to the people."

The Muslim leader is still negative, "Democracy won't help when they divide up the country. The European leaders have already made up their minds that this is the way to solve the problem."

The Croatian leader chimes in, "It is the only way they know how to deal with us. Divide us up. They can't let us live together. We're victims no matter what we do."

Vladimir counters their argument, "And where did you get that little bit of information?"

The Muslim leader and the Croatian leader say at the same time, "Belgrade TV." They both look at each other.

Vladimir raises his eyebrows, "Consider the source. What Belgrade TV is telling you is a lie. Belgrade TV is Jovanovic's propaganda machine."

The two leaders do a double take, and the Croatian leader mumbles, "Oh, my God!"

Vladimir presses the point, "You're playing right into the hands of the Serbs. You're doing exactly what they want you to do. As long as you are divided, the Serbs will take the majority of everything. Don't forget the quote you taught me of Lord Acton, 'Power tends to corrupt; absolute power corrupts absolutely. Great men are almost always bad men.' You taught me that we have a choice to do the right thing or be corrupt like all the other bad leaders. If you do the right thing and end the killing, the UN will see you as real leaders. They will back your request to go back to the pre-war land status If you can stand together and force a democratic solution, the Serbs can get no more than 19%."

The argument start to grow more and more heated. It is like they are not listening to what Vladimir is telling them.

The Croatian leader argues, "That might've been true two years ago, but now so many've been killed or forced to leave that we've no choice."

The Muslim leader argues, "We can't turn back the clock and hold elections based on where people lived two years ago."

Vladimir is vehement, "Why not? That's what you should insist on in the peace negotiations."

The Croatian leader answers, not seeing that the murder of his people is his strongest case, "Because those people are dead or gone. Now all that matters is that the Muslims agree that Mostar will be under Croatian control."

The Muslim leader blows a fuse, "Never! Right now all that matters is that the Croats agree that Mostar 'l be under Muslim control."

The Croatian leader shouts, "Never! We'll die first."

The Muslim leader shouts back, "And we'll be happy to oblige you. You wanna die. We don't care."

Vladimir steps back shaking his head. He tries to talk over their harangue, "You guys are hopeless. You're going to blow the only chance you may have!" But the men are so over the tope they talk right over top of everything Vladimir is saying.

The Croatian leader fires out, "And we don't give a damn how many of your homes get destroyed. One of us has to go, and it's gonna be you."

The Muslim leader fires back, "Oh, yea! We'll see about that!"

Vladimir walks out before they finish.

The Croatian leader fires back, "Well, it won't be us!"

Who knows how long this continued.

CHAPTER 34
Refugee Camp Sweden

Jusuf and Aisha are together again and fortunate enough to leave the war behind them. They have nothing but the clothes on their backs. They are displaced souls, who suddenly belong nowhere. The weeks drag into months as they are shuffled from one holding camp to another. In many countries, the lack of bribe money can slow the process down indefinitely. Fortunately, Jusuf's positive nature and Aisha's charm are a big help, so they at least remain active on the list. The hardest thing is the not knowing month to month.

Then finally, they find themselves on the last leg of their journey. The Red Cross assigns them to a refugee camp in a small village called Lomma, on the southwest coast of Sweden. The camp lies right on the beach overlooking the straits between Sweden and Denmark. It is a beautiful peaceful place. There are seventy-five cabin shelters, which are laid out like a small village. Each shelter has small private rooms.

Their buses come slowly up the main road and then turn down into the temporary refugee camp. A Croatian woman comes out of her office with a clipboard. She immigrated to Sweden years ago and is now a Swedish citizen and the camp Director.

The bus opens its door and people start to step down in awe. Each refugee feels overwhelmed by his or her new surroundings and temporarily paralyzed as their feet touch the Swedish soil. The Director checks their name on the list and assigns each person to their shelter. The people step away slowly, with their heads and bodies turning in all directions, trying to take in the panorama. They feel like they just went through hell and emerged in paradise.

Outside the gate, a group of Swedes is gathering. The look on their faces is unhappy and stern. There is no visible or vocal sign of protest, but it is obvious that they are not a welcoming party.

Aisha and Jusuf get off the bus together. The Director gives them their shelter assignment, and they walk a few meters toward the beach. Aisha is now in her perfect fantasy world. They stand gazing out at the water.

Aisha exclaims, "Isn't the world a grand place?"

Jusuf's eyes scan the full visible length of the waterfront before responding, "This is more like a vacation resort than a refugee camp. Mama, do you mind if I go for a walk on the beach?"

"Go, go! You deserve it; I'll get us settled in our room."

Aisha only has a small bundle of clothes and personal effects collected from the Red Cross over the past eight months. She makes her way to the shelter and finds the small room she and Jusuf will occupy. It has bunk beds, a small table with a chair and what to her is a large one-meter clothes cupboard. She smiles at how clean and nice everything is. To her amazement, the shelter also has a small bathroom with a toilet, sink and shower. Plus, it has a small cooking area to make tea of coffee. The sign on the cabinet says, "All meals will be served in the dining hall." The

sheet of paper next to it is the menu for the week. She
reads it carefully, meal by meal, day by day. When she
finishes, she stands staring at it.

Tears are filling Aisha's eyes. Her memory
flashes back to their treatment in the detention camp
at home. She can't help but think, "This is more food
in a day than we got in a month." She remembers
Meho's funeral and can see his burial. For the first
time, she sees it clearly and says, "My darling, you
don't need to worry about us anymore. Everything is
going to be grand again. I love you!"

As Jusuf walks on the beach, he watches the
small waves roll up on the sand. At one spot, he
discovers a small ledge in the sand, washed out by the
moving water. He stops and looks out across the
water and watches the setting sun. There is a peace
and calm that comes into his body now. His face is
glowing and his eyes are distant. Then his mind
makes a sudden leap into the world of Nedjo's riddle
of leadership.

Jusuf freezes on the edge of the sandy ledge
looking down at the shore along the water's edge.

Jusuf sees Vladimir on the cliff looking down
at the wolf and the lamb. His feet are naked and
frozen. Vladimir turns and looks directly at him. His
face is filled with peace and calm. Jusuf reaches out a
hand and puts it on his shoulder with reassurance. He
pulls Vladimir closer and embraces him. The tears
role down Jusuf's cheeks. He knows what his friend
must do. Vladimir pulls back, smiling. He holds his
friend at arm's length for a moment, and they look
into each other's eyes. Then, with a sigh, Vladimir

lets go and takes out his knife. He holds it up to the sky by the blade, as if in prayer. Then he sits on a snow covered stone, and bends down and takes hold of his right leg. There is only a slight wince in his face as he cuts off his frozen foot.

He picks up his foot and jumps from the cliff. He lands directly in front of the wolf, who snarls and growls at him, while holding tightly to the crying lamb. Vladimir offers the wolf his severed foot.

The look on the wolf's face changes. Vladimir kneels down still holding out his foot. The wolf lets go of the lamb, and it runs free. The wolf then sniffs the foot and licks the blood from it. He then eats the foot. His hunger is obvious.

Then the scene changes and Jusuf can see that Vladimir is walking with a stick under his arm. The wolf is at his side walking with him, and the lamb is following behind.

Jusuf takes a handkerchief from his pocket, wipes the tears from his face and blows his nose. He then turns and continues down the beach. The water is calm now, with only ripples lapping at the beach. The sun is sitting on the water and casting a golden beam on the surface directly to Jusuf. Jusuf sees a small white round and flat stone on the sand. He picks it up and holds it flat between his thumb and forefinger. He cocks his arm and says, "This is for you my friend." With one smooth motion and snap of the wrist, he throws the stone out across the water.

It skips upon the sunbeam seventeen times before sinking.

CHAPTER 35
Paradise Lost

In Hjärup, the neighboring community to Lomma, a group of people begins to gather in a meeting room. As they arrive, they engage in intense conversation. Some people are in a light mood and positive. However, there are many in a dark mood and negative. These people are borderline hostile.

Barely a week later, the camp Director approaches Jusuf with a mission. The camp Director believes Jusuf to be bright and articulate, so she invites him to attend a meeting in the nearby village of Hjärup. What Jusuf doesn't realize is that he is about to jump out of the frying pan and into the fire.

When they arrive, they stand for a moment and assess the situation. The meeting room is crowded with people, who by this time are engaged in heated conversations about the refugee situation. Then they walk over and sit on one side.

The camp Director whispers to Jusuf, "People may be a little upset, but they will not harm you. So don't be afraid."

Jusuf tries to confirm what he is hearing, "Are they protesting against setting up another refugee camp here?"

"Yes, but I hope you can help them see the need of the Bosnian people."

Two leaders move to the front of the room and take their places behind a table.

One of them, the leader of the majority party, calls the meeting to order, "Shall we begin?" The people settle down quickly. "I know you have a lot of questions and we'll get to them in a minute. But, first I want to give you some background.

"As you know, Sweden has agreed to take refugees from the former Yugoslavia. Each community is being asked to provide for their share of the total. So we have been asked to take 430 people into the proposed refugee camp outside Hjärup. You have all seen the plans for the camp, which shall provide a very nice environment for the refugees and produce a minimum of disruptions for the community. I hope that once we have answered your questions, you will be able to support your community leaders in this humanitarian effort. So let's begin with your questioning."

The leader points to an angry woman, with her hand up.

She stands. Her body and voice shaking with anger, "Hjärup is just a bedroom community. Who will protect our homes while we are away during the day? You know that you can't trust foreigners!"

An angry man stands to speak and starts without waiting to be recognized. "I understand you want to put the camp right next to my business, so every time the refugees want to take the train they will have to walk up my gravel road. Who is going to pay me when they have worn out the road?"

Another resident stands and speaks calmly, "Whatever happened to the kind and caring Swedes that I thought I lived with? Why aren't we united in the face of such a tragedy against humanity? The people in Bosnia-Herzegovina need our help."

As the resident sits down, the person sitting next to him leans over and threatens him, "If you know what's good for you, you'll keep your mouth shut!"

The resident is shocked.

An elderly man stands. "Hjärup is too small to have 430 refugees right next to us. We have only one small store, a library, a bank and a post office. What will the refugees do all day?"

A young student stands and waits to be recognized. "You're my elders, and I'm embarrassed. You make me ashamed to be living in Hjärup. What the world needs is more love and kindness, not anger, willful ignorance and distrust. We need understanding reason, not irrational nationalism. Didn't you get enough of that during the last war?"

The student is shouted and booed down.

The elderly man shouts, "Respect your elders! Shut up and sit down!"

The angry man shouts, "Sweden is for Swedes!"

A person shouts, "Send the foreigners home! And the kid too!"

The angry woman shouts, "What's your name? Does your mother know you're out?"

The majority leader tries to bring the group back to order. The minority leader is amused by the proceedings.

The majority leader calls out, "O.K., O.K., let's keep this orderly."

The minority leader tells her, "Let 'em go."

The minority leader stands up and when they have quieted down, he says, "When Sweden comes into the EU we will have to open our borders to those who want to come here and work, and that will be good for Sweden. However, these refugees are only coming here for a free handout, and Swedes are the ones who will have to pay."

The majority leader reacts in amazement. The crowd gives him a resounding applause. The minority leader steps back.

The majority leader says to him, "What kind of double talk is that?"

She then tries to bring them back to order. "Order, please. Excuse me, order!"

Jusuf stands and waits to be recognized. He is nervous, but feels compelled to speak to those few sympathetic people, who are present. He also knows that the truth and reality are always stronger than the phantom boogeyman of accusations and innuendos.

The majority leader points to him when the crowd quiets down.

Jusuf says proudly and clearly, looking each of the angry people in the eye, "I am a refugee from Konjic. My father has been killed, and my mother and I have come here to recover from a brutal ethnic war. In Konjic, most of the people have no homes. There is no heat or electricity. There is no food. We have endured this for the past two years and now the people need your help. If we could, we would work to pay our own way, but your rules do not allow us to do that. We just need a place to stay until we can heal physically and emotionally before we go back."

The angry woman interrupts without listening, "You can go back tomorrow. You're not wanted here."

The crowd joins in and cuts Jusuf off completely. The crowd quickly turns into an angry mob.

A person shouts, "Now they wanna take our jobs."

The elderly man yells, "I thought this was a meeting for Hjärup residents. What's he doing here?"

The camp Director takes Jusuf by the arm and they move through the crowd to get out. As they leave the meeting room, the prevailing mood of the mob is one of hatred, fear and hysteria. They are the same as any other mob anywhere else in the world.

To Jusuf, Sweden is paradise. But, he also knows that in any paradise there are the seeds of destruction. His hope for Sweden is that these Swedes never become the majority, or the fate of Sweden will be the same as Bosnia-Herzegovina.

CHAPTER 36
Power and Corruption

Back at the command center in the hills overlooking Konjic, Jovanovic has been conducting an inspection of Ranko's command. He has already inspected the troops and given them a pep talk, mostly to reverse the damage caused by Vladimir. Unfortunately, for him, the men are savvy now and his propaganda is a hard sell. As usual, Jovanovic's hidden agenda is not obvious.

Right now, Ranko and Jovanovic are deep in a discussion about command protocol regarding Ranko's living accommodations during the war.

Jovanovic tries to close the discussion, "Anyway that is the reason for this inspection of your command."

Ranko persists and reframes his position, "I don't think you understand. I need to have my estate intact. It is the only place clean enough to take a shower. I need to get away from the men. Their smell has become more and more repulsive. Just the thought of using the same latrine makes me constipated."

Jovanovic explains again, "I'm telling you it's an embarrassment. The men are living in trenches and you in absolute luxury. O.K., an officer should have privileges. So set up your own private quarters, your own private latrine. But what does it look like to the men and the press, if your estate's the only place that goes untouched by the war?"

Ranko counters, "Nedjo's home has gone untouched."

Jovanovic laughs. "Sure, and you're going to tell me there's a curse on anyone who touches your estate. If it makes you feel any better, bomb him out."

Ranko responds quickly, "No thank you, I'd rather keep my eyesight. I happen to know the curse is real. I actually saw what happened to the Germans, a whole bloody platoon."

Jovanovic is emphatic, "Its appearances pure and simple. No one gives a rat's ass about Nedjo. But as long as your estate is untouched the UN and the press will wonder why. When this is over, you'll have the funds to rebuild, twice as big and twice as elegant."

Ranko caves in, "O.K., but what do I do with Ana? Vladimir can live in the trenches with the men."

A dark demonic expression comes into Jovanovic's face, and he says, "That brings me to another point. Ana has served her usefulness. Your blood lines are unclean, pure and simple. She is Croatian. Dispose of her."

Ranko says without emotion, "I thought that you and Ana were..."

On this subject, Jovanovic leaves no opening for a discussion, "I don't give a damn what you thought. She's a liability. Vladimir's a liability. He is an enemy in our own camp. If you're not 100% Serbian, you're not to be trusted. Dispose of him, before he destroys everything. Dispose of them both!"

"Do you know what you're asking me to do?"

Jovanovic looks him square in the eye and smiles, "I not only know what I'm asking. I know you'll enjoy doing it. I've every confidence you'll be clever in pulling it off. See that it gets done."

Ranko grins and nods his head in the affirmative repeatedly.

CHAPTER 37
Doing the Unthinkable

That afternoon, on the Rakic estate, Ranko is standing in the middle of the front room of the house directing traffic. Vladimir and Ana are the traffic, each picking up the objects that Ranko points out, and then carrying them out the door to the back hall. They quickly return each time. Ranko is excessively authoritative.

Vladimir and Ana are moving all the household valuables into a secret vault in the basement. They take only those items that he indicates. They have no clue as to what Ranko is doing.

Ana asks, "Why must we put my jewelry in the basement? I'll have to go down there every time I need something."

Ranko says, "Which is better: to have it safe or have it where any garbage can get at it, if we get attacked?"

Vladimir asks, "Why can't the servants help us? I have other things to do."

"I let 'em go for the day. Do you want 'em to know about the secret vault?" Ranko says matter-of-factly.

In the family room, Vladimir starts to take down his Roman Empire war theatre.

Ranko commands him, "Leave that!"

"No way! You said we should take everything of value. This is priceless. Jusuf and I spent seven years building it, and it is the only thing I have left to remember him by."

Ranko turns away, grinning. He says to pacify him, "O.K., we'll take it last, if there's room. Start taking paintings."

Ann starts to take down some inexpensive erotic prints.

Ranko orders her, "Leave those. Take the valuable ones."

Ana protests, "Who's deciding what's valuable here? These give me pleasure."

"I am, and it's not open for debate!" Ranko covers, with a lighter attitude, "Besides, we gotta have somethin' on the walls to enjoy."

Ana is boiling with anger. It is all she can do to contain herself.

Ranko hands a sculpture he is holding to Vladimir.

Vladimir carries the sculpture to the basement vault. When he has left, Ranko calmly walks over to Ana.

He orders her, "Take that antique Chinese vase."

She picks it up and deliberately drops it. It falls to the floor and shatters into a million pieces. She stands there in defiance. He stands directly in front of her, calm and cool. He swings, with a fist, and hits her on the side of her face, sending her sprawling. He walks slowly over to her and kicks her, as she is trying to get up. She flies backward and smashes into one of the tables, and he kicks her again.

Vladimir comes back in and sees what his father is doing. He springs into action and pulls his father away. They struggle for a moment, and then Ranko calms down.

He holds up his hands in surrender, "O.K.! O.K., you can let me go now."

Vladimir goes to his mother and helps her up.

Ranko containing his rage and pointing his finger at Ana and then at Vladimir, "Pull one more stunt like that, I'll kill you. And you, interfere once more, I'll kill you too. Get back to work!"

Ranko picks something up and carries it down to the vault.

Vladimir and Ana make several trips, silently and reluctantly doing what he says. The house is stripped of everything valuable. Soon it looks almost vacant. At the end Vladimir tries to take his war theatre again. Ana starts to help. She can see how much it means to him.

Vladimir says, "Thank you, Mom. It is important to me."

Ranko returns and watches them for a moment. He now has an automatic weapon slung over his should and is carrying a small box. He tells them, "There ain't room for that. I've locked the vault. Come here."

Ana and Vladimir don't move. Ranko becomes annoyed, but says nothing. He shifts the box into one hand and starts to reach for the weapon.

Vladimir and Ana both see the movement toward the weapon and instantly drop what they are doing and silently walk over and stand in front of Ranko.

Ranko hands them spray-paint cans that he takes from the box, and tells them, "Write 'Damn Chetnik' on the walls with these spray-paint cans. Or anything else a garbage heathen might write."

Vladimir is suspicious, "What for?"

Ana doesn't have a clue yet, "How do you expect us to live here?"

Ranko barks, "That's an order! Write 'Crazy Nationalist Serb.'"

Vladimir rebels, "No way. I know what you're trying to do."

Ranko swings his automatic weapon around from his back and levels it at them.

Vladimir and Ana reluctantly follow his instructions. Ana writes, "PROKLETI CETNICI" and "DO DAVOLA VELIKA SRBIJA," but slowly she begins to remember a similar deception. Vladimir writes, "ISTINA CE POBIJEDITI."

Ana now realizes, "This is what you did at the library. My god, you destroyed the library. You bastard that was all I had left to remember my mother by."

Vladimir feels remorse and turns to his mother, "I'm sorry. I didn't know."

After a moment, Ana stops painting and slowly turns to face Ranko. Her face is filled with a new revelation and anger. She shouts, "This is what you did to my mother and father in Belgrade!"

Ranko stares at her for a moment, and then an evil smile comes to the corner of his mouth, "It sure took you long enough to figure that out."

"You're an evil monster!" She shouts and throws her paint can at him.

Vladimir turns to his father, with a shocked expression on his face. Ana races toward Ranko, but he opens fire. Her body flies backward to the ground.

Vladimir screams, "Nooooooo!"

Vladimir runs toward his mother, but Ranko cuts him down before he can reach her. He then sprays the walls and ceiling with bullets. Bits of furniture and plaster fly everywhere. He sprays Vladimir's Roman Empire war theatre, and it flies in all directions. Finally, he tips over an empty glass china cabinet on top of Vladimir. As it falls, a broken pane of glass falls to the floor, cutting off Vladimir's foot. His body is motionless.

In the distance, the sound of sirens can be heard.

Ranko runs out the back of the house and up into the woods above the estate. A group of UN Peace Keepers' vehicles comes speeding up the driveway toward the house.

No sooner has Ranko made his escape than the UN vehicles pull up in front of the house. Nedjo scrambles out of one of the vehicles. He fumbles for the controls of his vision device, but he has forgotten to bring it.

Nedjo calling out, "Vladimir. Vladimir!" He turns to the sergeant getting out of the other side of the vehicle. "Something's wrong, I tell you. I can feel it."

The sergeant reassures him, "I know. I believe you. That's why we're here."

They listen for a response, but there is none. The silence is chilling Nedjo to the bone. However, the UN peacekeepers, from Sweden, move much more cautiously.

Nedjo asks urgently, "Check out the house. I know something's happened to Vladimir."

"We'll take a look." The sergeant motions to his men. They cautiously move to the front door, which is open a crack, and enter. Half of them check the first floor; the other half climb up the center steps, with their weapons at the ready.

One of the UN soldiers comments, "What a mess!"

His buddy responds, "Looks like the Muslims finally took this place."

Another peacekeeper finds the two dead bodies, and pulls the china cabinet off Vladimir. When he sees the severed foot and a pool of blood, he is sickened and turns away.

He then goes to the door and shouts down, "Sarge, the boy and his mother are dead. They're lying up here."

Nedjo ask the sergeant, "Can you take me to the boy?"

The Sergeant leads him up the center steps and guides him through the ruble to where Vladimir's body lies and describes what he sees. "There is a bullet hole in his arm and two in his chest. He is lying in a pool of blood, which is mostly from his foot." He reacts. "It has been severed off."

"I've heard enough." Nedjo kneels down and feels the side of his neck for a pulse.

The sergeant locks on. "There's no way that he could still be alive."

Nedjo quickly picks him up and thrusts him into the sergeant's arms "Well, he is alive! And we have to get him to the hospital at once."

Vladimir's head turns and he coughs.

The sergeant exclaims, "Good God!" He turns and runs down the center stairs to the first floor, calling for his men to follow. He rushes out the front door and heads for the vehicle, with Nedjo holding on to his belt and stumbling along behind him.

The sergeant gets in the vehicle holding Vladimir and calling to his men, "Move it, we have to get to the hospital fast!' He turns to Nedjo, now sitting next to him, and hands him his bandana. "Quick, Help me! We have to stop the bleeding from the leg."

Nedjo responds immediately, and, by feel, ties the bandana below Vladimir's knee as a tourniquet. He then uses his own handkerchief to cover the end of the wound and help slow down the blood flow.

Meanwhile, the UN vehicles speed off to the hospital with their sirens blasting.

CHAPTER 38
A Medical Miracle

When they get Vladimir to the hospital in Konjic, they are able to stabilize his condition and remove the bullet in his arm, but they are not able to do the chest sugary to remove the two bullets that are too close to his heart. Through their contacts in the UN and Sweden, the sergeant and Nedjo were able to have him admitted as an emergency patient to the Lund hospital in Sweden.

There, an internationally known heart surgeon removed the two bullets close to his heart. All his bullet wounds are now healing nicely. Thanks to the quick first aid and lack of infection, they were able to save all of the leg above the ankle. However, Vladimir has not regained consciousness since the shooting.

There are nurses, orderlies and doctors moving about the ward where Vladimir is under care. They are checking patents, dispensing pharmaceuticals, making up beds and assisting where needed.

A nurse, who is coming on duty, stops one of the doctors, and asks, "Doctor? Do you have a minute?"

"Yes, nurse. What is it?"

"I was wondering how it is going with the Yugoslavian boy? I've been off for the last three days, and I notice that he is not in his bed."

The doctor responds, "He is still in a coma, and we can't find any medical reason for it. They have taken him down for a CAT scan, and he should be back up any time now."

The nurse suggests, "Maybe it's the trauma. God knows what he's been through there."

The doctor nods his head, "Could be. I think we'll just have to wait and see."

The doctor goes into a patient's room, and the nurse makes her way to the nurse's station.

After a while, an orderly wheels Vladimir off the elevator and down the hall, on a gurney. As he wheels the gurney past the nurse's station, he motions to the nurse, who smiles and joins him. They take him into his room and the nurse and orderly lift him over on to the bed. They secure his side rails and leave.

When they wheel Vladimir in, Nedjo is asleep in a chair next to the bed. He is exhausted. When he hears the side rails clank into place, he starts to wake up. Nedjo has not left his side for the past week.

Vladimir starts to stir and mumble in his sleep.

Nedjo is awake in a second. He quickly puts on his vision device and looks at him for a moment. He gets up and goes to him, takes his hand to hold it and looks down into his face. He reaches down to smooth back Vladimir's hair.

As Vladimir starts to regain consciousness, he finds himself in complete darkness. He can see absolutely nothing. Yet he can feel that he is standing in a massive sea of humanity. He cannot see anyone, but he can feel all the bodies pressing in against him. He feels them being shoulder to shoulder, back to chest and chest to back. It feels like this unseen mass of people is pressing in on him tighter and tighter.

He tries to climb above them, to free himself from them. But each of them is also trying to climb above everyone else. In the blackness, it is madness. It is futile. It is meaningless. Without thinking, he relaxes, and his body seems to melt into the earth beneath the feet of the masses.

The darkness then becomes an infinite emptiness in which he is floating. He feels a sense of peace unlike anything he has felt before. It is so tranquil, he wants to bathe in it for the rest of eternity.

Then he sees a white speck appear in the darkness. It is like a speck of lint on a dark piece of cloth. He reaches out to flick it away, but his finger passed through it. He looks again and sees that it is a speck of light.

He reaches out and cradles the speck of light in the palm of his hand. Now he can see his hand in the darkness. The speck of light grows larger and brighter. He can now see his arm and chest. And the light grows even larger and brighter still.

Now the light is so bright he cannot see his hand or any part of himself. In fact, he can feel the light all around him and within him. He can feel an overwhelming sense of joy. He can feel something he never felt before, a caring and calming feeling, a soft and gentle touch, a hand that is cradling his heart and him. Out of that light, he hears a voice, "I am here within you." That is when he realizes that he has died and gone to heaven.

Slowly, Vladimir opens his eyes. He tries to bring the heavenly place into focus. The light is so bright it is blinding.

Yet, it is the sun streaming in the window, which is making everything look so bright and white. Gradually, Nedjo comes into focus.

Vladimir says weakly, "I always knew you were an angel!"

Nedjo smiles, "I'm not an angel."

Vladimir's face starts to brighten with interest. "Where am I?"

"You're in Lund, Sweden…"

"Don't tell me. The doctor's your personal friend." Vladimir cuts him off.

Nedjo laughs, "No, no, he's a personal friend of a personal friend."

Vladimir laughs, but it hurts. He grabs his chest and grimaces from the pain.

Nedjo squeezes his hand, "You have to take it easy."

"How long have I been here?"

"About a week now."

Vladimir has a sudden realization, "My mom!"

He starts to get up swinging his legs out of bed, but the pain is too great.

Nedjo helps him lay back, "Your mom is dead."

Vladimir sinks back across the bed mumbling, "That poor stupid bastard."

Nedjo says, not understanding, "You shouldn't blame Jusuf for what other Muslims have done."

Now Vladimir is confused, "Why should I blame Jusuf? Besides, he's probably dead by now. The Muslims didn't do this. My father did!"

Nedjo is shocked. He helps Vladimir move his legs back onto the bed, and Vladimir sees that his foot is gone. He looks at it for a moment and then looks up at Nedjo. Nedjo shrugs his shoulders.

Nedjo says, "The wolf?"

Vladimir smiles saying, "Then he's been fed."

Nedjo is amazed, "You know the meaning of the riddle!"

Vladimir's face becomes very sad and tears well up in his eyes. His head sinks back into his pillow.

After a moment he says, "It hurt a lot more to lose my best friend."

CHAPTER 39
The Search

As the days pass, Vladimir grows stronger and stronger. He jokes with the nurses and other patents. He is joyful and positive. Right now, a nurse is helping Vladimir, who is trying to walk on crutches down the hall. He cheerfully struggles with his handicap. Within a matter of minutes, Vladimir hands one crutch to the nurse and walks easily with only one.

At the same time, Nedjo is busy with plans of his own. While wearing his vision device, he is looking out the window of a train as it pulls into Stockholm central station.

With a map in his hand, Nedjo begins to walk up a side street in front of the station. When he reaches the walking street, he turns to the right and walks toward Old Town. He crosses one bridge, walks through the arches of the government buildings and crosses another bridge.

Nedjo is a man with a mission. He searches for a street on the map and then hurries on. He approaches the King's palace near Old Town. After speaking to the guard, who knows him, he knocks and a butler, who also knows him, escorts him in. The Butler leads him to the King's chambers.

King Carl Gustaf and Queen Silvia warmly greet Nedjo. The royal children are also anxious to meet him. They are served coffee and cake. But soon their discussion turns to a serious matter, and the King picks up the phone and makes an inquiry. He then writes something on a piece of stationery, folds it and hands it to Nedjo, who is most grateful. Nedjo then says goodbye and continues his mission.

Back at the hospital, Vladimir is being fitted with prosthesis. The doctor explains how it works. Vladimir tries it out, but has some difficulty. The doctor takes it into his laboratory, inviting Vladimir to come along. He makes some adjustments on the artificial foot, and Vladimir tries it again. With the aid of a walker for balance, Vladimir is able to walk.

In Stockholm, Nedjo has made his way to the Office of Swedish Immigration. He is greeted by a friendly official. He hands her the note on the royal stationery. She reads it and smiles broadly at Nedjo. She searches for something in her computer. After several tries, she finds it. She writes something down on the back of the paper and hands it to Nedjo. He thanks her and leaves.

Vladimir is walking, without any aid and with only a little difficulty. As he passes nurses and doctors, they greet him. Other patients, standing in the hall, greet him as he approaches.

He is making his way down the corridor to the dining area. Vladimir is very cheerful. He ends up looking out the window in the dining area and sees the blowing wind and rain. Then his face becomes serious and distant.

In his mind, he can see himself as a child playing with Jusuf on one of their many adventures. He sees the moment when they pledged their loyalty to each other for life. He sees their hysterical laughter over something they said or did.

Now Nedjo's mission becomes clear. He has found the refugee camp in Lomma. Yes, he knows the camp Director very well. She then leaves Nedjo in the office, and he watches her run through the rain to one of the cabins. In a moment, she comes out with another woman and the two women run back to the office.

As they come in, Aisha takes off the scarf covering her head. Both, she and Nedjo, are thrilled to see each other. They hug hard. Nedjo then explains something to Aisha, who becomes more and more emotional. Her excitement is obvious as Nedjo lays out a plan in detail. By the time he finishes, Aisha is bouncing with anticipation.

Only a half hour later, Nedjo joins Vladimir at the window in his room and admires the prosthesis. Vladimir is overjoyed to demonstrate his new foot as he prances around the room.

The following morning is a beautiful spring day, and Nedjo and Vladimir are standing at the window in the ward's dining area. Nedjo is pointing across the farmland to a small wooded area called Dalby Hage. He explains that through the woods are many walking paths, and asks if he is up for a little outing.

Vladimir listens and nods his head in agreement. This will be his first outing since he arrived in Lund. Just the thought of feeling the sun on his face has him jumping out of his skin.

At the same time, Aisha is explaining the same thing to Jusuf.

Jusuf listens and nods his head in agreement. He thinks it sounds like an adventure. He has never seen a virgin wood before, except maybe in the Fairytale.

Nedjo takes Vladimir in a cab to Dalby Hage and the main entrance to the park.

The camp Director chauffeurs Aisha and Jusuf to the back entrance of the park.

In the virgin wood of Dalby Hage the trees are in their early spring foliage and the forest floor is covered with wild flowers of many kinds. It is a magical place as old as time itself. Soon Nedjo and Vladimir approach an ancient stone road that runs through the heart of the wood. It is a narrow road, with round cobblestones covered with moss. Vladimir is walking almost normally now, with barely a limp.

When he sees the road, he stands in awe. He turns to Nedjo, saying, "It's like we just walked into the Fairytale."

Nedjo responds, "I assure you, it's very real."

On the other side of the wood, Aisha and Jusuf approach the other end of the ancient road.

Jusuf asks, "Are you sure that this is real, or have I gone into the Fairytale again?

Aisha says, "It looks real to me, but you know how I am."

Jusuf looks down the road. "It feels like..., as if I were to walk down that road, I would meet a prince on a gallant steed."

Aisha says, "You go ahead. I forgot some tissue. I'll catch up.

Aisha heads back to the car.

Vladimir also says, "That's weird, I can picture a knight on a white horse coming down that road. This is just like the Fairytale."

Nedjo says, "This is too beautiful to pass up. I'm going back to the cab for my camera. Why don't you start down the road, and I'll catch up."

Nedjo heads back to the cab.

Thus, the two boys are set on a journey on the same road. As they walk along, they marvel at the beauty of the flowers and the trees. Each pinches himself to make sure he is not in the Fairytale. After a while, they each can see the other at a distance. But before they are close enough to recognize each other, they put their heads down and walk along as though they were meeting a stranger. When they are only about five meters apart, they each look up into the face of the friend they thought was dead.

They freeze in disbelief. Then they speak at the same time.

"Vladimir?"

"Jusuf?"

They run toward each other. There is a long hug, with lots of backslapping.

Jusuf says, "I thought you were dead."

Vladimir holds Jusuf at arm's length, "I thought **you** were dead."

They pull back and look at each other.

Vladimir smiles, "You're not an old man!"

Jusuf smiles, "And you're not so big, without your armor!"

They BOTH laugh and start to walk back up the road. They have their arms around each other's shoulders. They walk in silence. Every now and then, they stop and look at each other. At one point, they punch each other lightly in the shoulder to make sure that all this is real. Then they both laugh.

CHAPTER 40
Sunset

The next day the Boys meet at the refugee camp and go for a walk on the beach in Lomma. Mostly they walk in silence and enjoy the present moment of being back together again. One day they will tell each other their personal stories about the war, but right now, they are basking in the glory of their eternal friendship. Right now, everything they see, everything they hear, everything they experience is a new adventure.

As they walk on the beach, they come upon a large driftwood log. They study it together, discuss where it has been and imagine what it has seen. Finally, they sit down on the log.

Nedjo stands watching them from a distance.

The two boys sit quietly watching the sunset on the beach. The silence is filled only with the sounds of the waves and the distant bells on the buoys. Finally they have found peace and calm. They have found a feeling of tranquility. They have escaped the war and nightmare through which they have come.

Vladimir turns to Jusuf, and says, "You know we must go back.

Jusuf says calmly, "I know." He pauses while staring at the sunset. "We will do it together."

After a moment, Vladimir asks, "How can we organize a resistance against the killing and destruction?"

Jusuf asks, "Do you remember what a person is called when he commits crimes against society without feelings?"

"Ah... sociopaths or psychopaths, I think."

"That's it."

Vladimir adds, "But most people aren't like that."

Jusuf agrees, "Exactly, it's only the power-hungry military leaders and phony politicians."

Vladimir says, "That's why there's no diplomatic or political solution that can bring about change."

Jusuf reflects, "The way I see it, the only lasting change will have to come from the people."

Vladimir jumps on the idea, "You're right. The people must take the responsibility upon themselves."

Jusuf continues, "We must change the hearts of our people, so they can fight the sickness in our society."

Vladimir comes up with the sound bite, "A world without prejudice and hatred is a world without war. Like the wolf, the people need to be fed."

Jusuf nods his head, "Our resistance shall feed them. Then the psychopaths will be generals without armies and politicians without fools to follow them."

"Do you think Nedjo will help us?" Vladimir asks.

Jusuf stares at the golden beam spreading across the water and sees his skipping stone. He says confidently, "I think **we** can do it."

Vladimir says, "You know, we could be killed."

Jusuf says, "I would rather die believing in love and kindness, than live my life in the gray zone of willful ignorance, doubt and skepticism."

Nedjo smiles, he can tell by their body language the decision they made, and he knows they are up for the task.

 As the Boys are left illuminated in the setting sun, the lights flash in their brains and the Fairytale scene appears.

The Young Prince and the Old Carpenter are sitting on a log looking out over the water, and their backs are silhouetted against the setting sun. They think to themselves, maybe  one day the world will live happily ever after.

The Boys look at each other and smack high-five. They both shout at the same time, "**It ended!**"

The Fairytale is released from their minds. But, the message and lessons it gives them will live forever in their hearts.